MODERN ART

EVELYN TOYNTON

MODERN ART

A NOVEL

DELPHINIUM BOOKS

HARRISON, NEW YORK   ENCINO, CALIFORNIA

FIC
TOY

All rights reserved under
International and Pan-American Copyright Conventions.
Published in the United States by
DELPHINIUM BOOKS, INC.,
P.O. Box 703, Harrison, New York 10528.

ALL THANKS TO MJA.

Library of Congress Cataloging-in-Publication Data
Toynton, Evelyn.
Modern art / by Evelyn Toyton— 1st Ed.
p. cm
ISBN 1-883285-18-6
1. Traffic accident victims—Family relationships—Fiction.
2. Biography as a literary form—Fiction. 3. Painters' spouses—Fiction.
4. Widows—Fiction. I. title.
PS3570.O97 M6 2000
813'.54—dc21   00-024570

First Edition
10 9 8 7 6 5 4 3 2 1

Distributed by HarperCollins Publishers
Printed in the United States of America on acid-free paper

Book design by Krystyna Skalski

For GDT

MODERN ART

1

"MISS PROKOFF," THEY SAY, CAREFUL TO USE THE NAME
that appears on her paintings, "Miss Prokoff, can you tell us how . . .
can you tell us when . . . ?" And she does it, she tells them, although
she has answered these questions a hundred times before. For two
hours, on this April afternoon, she has been scrupulous about dates,
materials, techniques, even the brand of house paint he used in the
works of his middle period. They have transcribed her words
solemnly into their blue spiral notebooks with the Columbia crest.

Twenty years ago, they would have been wearing fuzzy angora
sweaters. Now they are dressed like torturers' apprentices, in mul-
tiple earrings and studded leather jackets, but with the same blond
cleanliness, that air of shining mental hygiene produced by a certain kind of affluent childhood. Being an old hand at this, Belle
knows that they are girding themselves to ask her another sort of
question, something personal, speculative, whose answer they can
tell to their friends.

"It must feel so amazing to paint in his studio," the more enter-
prising one says, leaning towards her. Belle ignores this remark, as
though she might be slightly deaf.

"Or it could be intimidating," the other one says helpfully. Belle
turns to look at her, admiring her pink-and-white skin. Nobody in
Brooklyn ever had skin like that; maybe it was the starchy food, or
the soot from the factories. She remembers years of oatmeal masks,

the little tubs of fatty cream she bought in secret from an old woman who made it in her kitchen — all that trouble and worry, in hopes of some transformation that never came. The one good thing about getting old is that it's finally all right to be ugly.

The first one tries again. "Didn't you sometimes feel intimidated by him? I mean . . . overwhelmed?"

"No." As they look at her wide-eyed, she moves her hands stealthily in her lap, to ease the pain.

"But wasn't it hard, both of you being painters? Do you think he ever felt you were competing with him?"

"No."

The girl gives a rueful laugh. "I wish I knew the right questions, Miss Prokoff, to get you to talk to us."

"If I'd felt threatened by him I wouldn't have married him. If I'd been competing with him he wouldn't have married me. We wouldn't have stayed together."

"But the art world was such a patriarchy then, everyone says so. No one took women artists seriously, did they?"

"He took me seriously," she says. It isn't true, of course; he wanted her for a nanny, a helpmeet, just as they suspect, but she has maintained this lie too long to start confiding in graduate students. Nor can she explain that it wasn't the patriarchal art world, it wasn't female diffidence that blighted her life, but the makers of Budweiser. Though stories of his drunkenness are legion, part of the mythology surrounding him, nobody has ever come right out and asked her, "What was it like to live with a drunk?"

"What do you know about the Federal Arts Project?" she says. The Arts Project should satisfy their craving for injustice — so many purges, investigations, the avant-gardists forced to do figurative work, the women assigned to gesso the walls for the men. They bow their heads again, frowning in concentration, and take copious notes for another half hour. Finally she tells them about the first time she saw his paintings, and then announces that it is time to leave.

Like obedient children, they shut their notebooks at once. In payment for this interview, they are driving her to the opening of a show she is having, in a small gallery here on the Island. The bolder of the two girls is a niece of Monica, the gallery owner; it was Monica who arranged for them to come and speak to Belle about their master's theses.

They get to their feet, looking expectant. "You're going to have to help me up," she says gruffly. "I've got very bad arthritis, I can't do it myself."

"My mother has it too," says Monica's niece, putting down her tote bag.

"Everyone's mother has it."

She takes Belle's out-stretched hand and tries to yank her up in one brisk movement, grunting when Belle falls back in her seat.

"You're not very good at this, are you?"

"I'm sorry."

"You try," Belle commands the other one, who manages, with a desperate effort, to haul her onto her feet. Now they both hover solicitously, exchanging little glances, but she refuses their help in getting to the car. It's horrible, being a dead weight like this, lifted and lowered and shepherded around. Nobody knows the foolishness she has stooped to in hopes of a cure — the spa in the Alps, shuffling between hot and cold springs all day; the clinic on the Upper East Side, where liquid gold was shot into her veins for weeks. That was the final humiliation, the height of decadence, but it would have been worth it if she'd gotten back the use of her hands. In her mind she is always painting, lying awake at night moving shapes from one side to another of the rectangle she sees in the dark. She might as well be blind for all the good it does her.

When they reach the car, they seat her in back, so she can put her leg up. The radio blasts out a pop song, and Monica's niece snaps it off quickly, in embarrassment.

"It's all right," Belle says, "turn it on." At first the girl protests, but then she tunes in again and a minute later seems to forget Belle is there.

"He's so retro, don't you think?" she says to her friend, jiggling to the music.

"Oh, but that's the whole point."

Belle likes them better now, stripped of their solemnity. And it is very soothing, after all, to go gliding along in this padded machine, staring out the window and watching the clouds change over the potato fields. "Look at nature": it was the only advice Cézanne would ever give. One of these days she will get herself a driver, she will go to the bluffs and sit there looking at the ocean. As it is, Nina, her daily help, must drive her around, and Nina does not feel she should get paid for looking at the ocean. The last time they went for a drive, Nina worried the whole way about a raccoon getting into the garbage.

On their arrival at the gallery, she takes the girls' arms after all, ascending between them into a roomful of people in polished high heels and striped silk jackets. In her baggy cotton dress, her canvas Topsiders, Belle might be mistaken for the maid, except that everyone there knows better. They all stand with drinks aloft, talking animatedly or darting looks around the room; no one pays any attention to her paintings, except for one frail-looking man in a beautiful black suit, a stranger to her, who is standing very close to the one she likes best, scrutinizing it intently from left to right and back again. She did these paintings, her last ones ever, to be looked at in just that way, examined for tiny brushstrokes and gradations of color.

She would like to talk to him, but she gets no chance. The others are crowding around her now, to kiss her cheeks and exclaim: associate curators, directors of publications, organizers of traveling exhibits. Those of the very highest rank could not be expected to travel all this distance in the off-season, but they have packed the room with their emissaries; one of them has even sent his wife. They're hoping she'll remember their museums in her will, though these, of course, are not the canvases they're after. In a temperature-controlled vault, inside an elaborately guarded warehouse in Queens, are fourteen late Maddens, the golden prize, the treasure she has stored against a lonely old age. As long as she owns those canvases, her telephone will go on ringing; half the people at the opening could probably name them all, with dates and dimensions.

"You look marvelous," they say brightly, "but not as marvelous as these," gesturing at the walls. Nothing she can say will deflect such flattery. She looks around for the girls who brought her, wondering if they are still taking notes, but she cannot locate them.

Instead here is Ernest, in a jaunty brown suit like a forties gangster's, looking like a death's head with his terrible false teeth. Nevertheless, she feels a great rush of fondness at the sight of him, a sort of gratitude that he should still be his finicky old self. It is one of the mysteries of her old age, this tenderness for Ernest, who used to goad her to fury every time he opened his mouth. Now the fussy precision of his speech, his air of laboring under the burden of his own importance, seem touching somehow, like a gallant refusal to admit defeat. Besides, he is the one person she can still bicker with, the only one who never tries to placate her.

She puts up her cheek to be kissed, takes him by the hand, and walks him away from the others. "Very rhapsodic," he says, nodding at the paintings.

"You've seen them before."

"I'm aware of that. I thought they were rhapsodic then too. A passionate farewell to the physical world."

"They are not. Anyway, that's *not* the kind of thing you say."

"I'm too old to be a formalist anymore. You too. These are your venture into metaphysics."

"That's ridiculous."

"Painters can never see their own work." He flicks a piece of lint from the shoulder of her dress. "How is your daily help faring these days?"

Twice recently, Nina has shown up for work with bruises on her face; the first time, she said she'd fallen down the cellar steps, while the second time she claimed to have walked into a door.

Everyone in the village knows about Nina's husband — his drug use, his paranoia, his brushes with the police — but when Belle tries to warn her, she says it's all lies, that nothing is wrong: now that they have a light on those steps, she'll be fine.

"He did it again last week. And she does not enjoy it, so don't start that."

"Would she tell you if she did? The real question is why you get so upset about it."

"Any time I feel compassion for someone, you think it's a sign of creeping senility."

"Only when there's a crazy husband involved. But perhaps that's not the point."

"What is the point, then? And keep your voice down."

He frowns; he purses his mouth. "I suspect you think of her as a simple peasant, and so you want to believe she must be happier than you are. It's the oldest fallacy around, you ought to know that by now. The inarticulate suffer, the untalented suffer, the ones who watch television suffer. It's insulting to them to think otherwise."

"You don't even know anybody who watches television."

"Nevertheless, I'm right."

"It isn't that. It's that she deserves to be happy."

"So do a lot of other unhappy people."

"Not the ones I meet." She cannot explain to him that Nina alone asks nothing from her. Nina only seems sad that anyone as rich and sought-after as Belle should get so little pleasure from it all.

"I suspect it's her cooking that makes you sentimental. It's terrible how much one cares about food at our age. I remember a very tasty lamb stew she made once. And speaking of that, are you going to dinner after this business? Is someone fêting you?"

"The gallery is."

"I trust I'm invited."

"Of course."

"Where are they taking us?"

She names the restaurant, and he nods in satisfaction.

"A very good wine list. Does dear Monica really expect to sell enough paintings to pay for such a bash?"

But she cannot summon up the snide response that seems called for. She has just been assailed by the dizziness that afflicts her lately, a falling in her stomach, as though crucial cells are dying off inside her. If she says to Ernest, "I am getting weaker, I am going to die," he will tell her they are all going to die, that Socrates too was mortal. She clutches at his arm. "Take me to the office, would you? I've got to sit down."

Suddenly she feels herself stagger, her knees give way, and Ernest wobbles dangerously, about to collapse under the pressure of her hand. They do a little dance, bobbing and tottering, until, with a desperate effort, she steadies herself, hauling him upright at the same time.

And then Monica is there, looking over Ernest's shoulder. "Are you all right?" she cries, in what seems like a very loud voice.

"She ought to get off her feet," Ernest says fretfully. "She almost fainted there for a minute." Belle turns to glare at him, but Monica's arm is around her shoulder, guiding her through the crowd.

"I'm perfectly okay," she says. "There's no need to fuss."

"Of course there isn't. But let me just take you to the office, where there's a nice soft couch." A minute later, Monica leaves her to fetch a glass of water, and Ernest appears in the doorway.

"You were some help," she snaps. For once he is silent. From this angle, looking up at him, she can see the folds of grizzled skin on his neck, which make her regret her unkindness. "Never mind. It wasn't your fault."

"I was quite strong in the old days," he says, clearing his throat. "For my size, anyway. People were always surprised at how athletic I was."

She shuts her eyes, remembering a sunny morning at Louse Point, a softball game among the artists, with Clay trying desperately to pitch the ball so that Ernest could hit it, bewildered that anyone as clever as Ernest was unable to perform so simple an act. Only Ernest, of all the players that day, had been unaware of what was happening, of the jokes and winks at his expense as he swung and swung, striking out both times at bat.

And she thinks, not for the first time, how fiercely Clay would have hated getting old, what a bad job he would have made of it. Acceptance, resignation, all those things would have eluded him; he would have gone on jumping off walls, throwing punches, diving into the ocean in January, until all his bones were broken and everyone around him was embarrassed by the spectacle. Five more years — maybe he could have lived that long, or even ten, if his luck had held, but in the end he would still have driven off a road somewhere. Endurance had never been one of his strong points.

2

"SHE THOUGHT WE WERE RIDICULOUS, YOU KNOW."

"Who did?"

"Miss Prokoff. I could tell."

"Well, it was her fault. She wouldn't give us any kind of a straight answer. I don't know why she said we could interview her if she didn't want to tell us anything."

"She's done it all a million times before, that's why."

"You always have to defend everyone, Lizzie, it makes me want to throw up. I thought she was an old bitch. And really, never mind feminism, could you stand to look like that? I'd rather be dead. Do you have any money on you?"

"About six dollars. I thought she was absolutely amazing, she was so fierce and alive and sort of unbowed. I kept thinking, God, I hope I can be like that when I'm old."

"I knew you'd make some big romance out of it. I've only got about three dollars, and that's counting change; we'll have to settle for McDonald's or something. I'm starving."

They, too, had been invited to the party after the opening, but Belle's dizziness had returned, along with wavy lines in front of her eyes, as soon as she stood up; in consequence, her celebration was deferred for a month, though some of the visitors from New York headed for the restaurant anyway. "I was counting on at least getting a decent meal out of my aunt," Heather says now, which is pretty much what the curators are saying about Monica over their drinks: "She could at least have told us to charge the dinner to her."

Only Lizzie is in an exalted frame of mind, a habitual state with her lately, after a winter of deep and unalterable gloom. "You ought to go on Lithium," is what Heather says, unfeeling as always, though Heather herself, just last fall, swallowed two hundred aspirin after a postdoctoral fellow in cultural studies ditched her for an associate professor. It was Lizzie who took her to the infirmary, Lizzie who brought her magazines and corn chips when she could sit up again. Though they grew up privileged, as Belle suspected, they are not unscathed, these two; there is a forlornness in each that the other sensed from the beginning.

"You can eat the whole nine dollars' worth," Lizzie says, "I've got to go on a diet," at which Heather tells her that she is probably anorexic on top of everything else. But this, at least, is not true; Lizzie has gained all of four pounds in the past two months, the result of happiness, and of eating Oreos in her lover's bed at three in the morning. Having grown up in Australia, and been weaned on aniseed sticks, the man she is in love with has a passion for the sugary treats of American childhood. America, he tells her sternly, is a Mickey Mouse country, but then so is Australia, and at least America has Oreos and Reese's Peanut Butter Cups and Mallomars.

She is pleased to be getting back early, so that she can call him that much sooner. Back in the apartment she shares with two other graduate students, she drags the phone into her bedroom for privacy, squatting on the dirty rug just inside the door, while in the living room her two roommates stare despondently at the television, as she used to do. The whiz of bullets mingles with the sound of ringing at the other end. Just when she has counted twelve rings, and is starting to worry, he picks up.

"It's me."

"So it is," he says, "so it is. Hang on a minute." There is the comforting, familiar sound of his single chair being scraped across the uneven floorboards of his loft. "Go ahead. I want to hear all about it."

"She was amazing," she says, in a rush. "Really wonderful.

Like someone who's lived through all the pain there is and come out the other side."

But he is silent, waiting, she knows, for news not of Belle Prokoff but Clay Madden, any gleanings she can offer — the sight of the splattered floorboards in his studio, an old drawing of his on the wall, a story his widow told that everyone doesn't know already — so he can hoard it to himself. Apart from junk food, Clay Madden is the chief justification he finds for the existence of America. When he was in art college, back in Melbourne — Lizzie would have been three years old — and the museum there bought a vast Madden that the taxpayers howled at the price of, he went and looked at it every day for a year. It was that painting that had made him abandon figuration, all those atmospheric landscapes and portraits that had already won him a modest reputation in his native city. "Mr. Doherty draws like an angel," said Sir Kenneth Clark, in town to give a lecture, and his remark was quoted throughout the school. After seeing the Madden, he stopped drawing like an angel. Belle Prokoff is not the chief point of interest.

"Did she have anything of his around?"

"No. There were a couple of hers on the wall. And then we went to her show. I don't know why you say her work is so bad. I think it's beautiful."

He snorts. "It's wallpaper. Pretty decorations. She probably can't afford to keep his paintings out there, the insurance would cost too much. Did she talk about him to you?"

"A little. Only when we pressed her. She told us about meeting him and said he'd always supported her work, stuff like that. You could tell she'd said it all a million times before. I felt like such a fraud, because she thought I was an art historian too. But I was really glad I went."

"Tell me exactly what she said about him."

"It's all stuff you know already. About how she went to see him because they were in some show together, she'd seen his name on the card and didn't know who he was, and then she was knocked out by the paintings. You told me that story yourself."

"Did you see his studio?"

"Yes."

"You lucky bugger. I'd give my left nut to get in that place."

"It's her studio now."

"I don't know how she can paint in there. Who was at the opening? A lot of honchos?"

"I guess. I wouldn't recognize them anyway."

"Did you all go out to some posh restaurant?"

"No. She almost fainted at the opening. She's old, you know, and she gets these dizzy spells. So the dinner was canceled. We went to a McDonald's on the way back." She waits for him to say, "When will I see you?" or "What are you doing tomorrow?" but the silence extends itself.

"Have you been working?" she asks finally.

"Of course I've been working; I've been changing the glaze on that red painting. It looks fucking beautiful now. Not that anyone will notice."

"Someone will notice," she says staunchly. "The people who know anything will." This is the role she has taken on, as bearer of hope, chief purveyor of consolation. And she believes everything she says — she has read all his clippings, every last word; she is convinced by the promise they hold forth. Some day there will be a new reckoning.

The last time he had a show, several months before she met him, three downtown painters wrote him admiring letters, telling him how much his work meant to them; the owner of a prestigious gallery spent half an hour in front of one canvas and then told his dealer, "Blood was sweated over this painting." A critic for an intellectual journal said it was "some of the most satisfying work I've seen this year . . . Paul Doherty is our most intelligent geometric abstractionist, one of the few contemporary painters able to give meaningful form to his obsessions." There was even a glowing review in *Art in America*.

But the *New York Times* said nothing, and only two small canvases sold. Lizzie, to whom he told the story the first time they went to bed, grieves over this fact even now, though she believes it is only a matter of time before things change for him. Meanwhile, the art world's refusal to grant him his due seems to her the single obstacle to their happiness.

She has had some experience in dealing with the inexplicable, being powerless to change what is clearly unfair. When she was fourteen, her mother was crossing the street in Stamford, on her way to a shop where they repaired old china, and got knocked down by a hit-and-run driver. The cracked Spode platter she was carrying smashed into a million pieces, and she was in a coma for a week. For two years after that, she was in and out of hospitals with mysterious seizures and spasms, until one of them killed her. But Lizzie still believes, as an article of faith, that one should always remain hopeful.

Anyway, there is nothing irrevocable about what has happened, or failed to happen, to Paul. Things could change any day, although sometimes, lying awake beside him, she is stricken by the thought that she has never seen him really happy, and maybe she never will.

Finally he remembers her. "So what are we doing tomorrow? Are you coming over?"

"If you want. I could bring something for dinner."

She will take the subway, changing several times, to the shabby neighborhood in Brooklyn where he lives surrounded by Polish butchers and Ukrainian bakeries. She will cook dinner on the one working burner on his hot plate, while Monteverdi plays loudly over the speakers, to drown out the heavy metal sounds from the loft up-stairs. Then they will smoke a joint and go to bed in the sealed-off freight elevator he has converted into his bedroom. Afterwards, in the middle of the night, they will pad around naked, licking chocolate off their fingers and looking at his paintings. At some point she will show him the letter she received this week from her old professor at Amherst. He had planned to go to

London this summer to do research for his book on Carlyle and the hermeneutic tradition. Now his wife has contracted Lyme disease, and he wonders if Lizzie could go in his stead. Ever since the letter arrived, she has been trying to think of a respectable reason for refusing; what worries her is that tomorrow, when she tells Paul about it, he may not plead with her to stay.

They agree that she should buy some shrimp to cook in his wok, he will pay her back, and now, the arrangements made, she can go peacefully to bed. Replacing the telephone on its wobbly perch in the living room, a stand that someone's mother once used for plants, she says good night to her roommates, who barely look up from the TV. Then she washes her face with the expensive black soap, made from mud and seaweed, that is her one remaining luxury, removes her contact lenses, and crawls between the covers with a copy of *Lolita* from the Columbia library. She has been anxious to read it because Lionel Trilling said it was about love, and love is all that interests her these days. Most of her mental life, in fact, consists of reflections on the subject. She has decided that Plato was right, that all her life she has been searching for the part of her soul left behind at birth, and now she has found it. No matter how often she has this revelation, it always retains its power to move her.

Paul Doherty does not know, because she keeps him from knowing, how much of her time is spent thinking about these matters; he believes that she, like him, has whole hours, days, when her mind is fixed entirely on what she is doing. She wouldn't tell him that even her mind is not her own these days. She has been taken over by a foreign power; what used to be her center has dissolved into a random collection of particles, held together only by consciousness of him.

Occasionally, coming up for air from some book she is reading, having forgotten him for three whole minutes, she wonders why the return of awareness does not please her, why it feels instead like a constriction in her heart muscles, a niggling uneasiness akin to pain. But even this thought seems like a betrayal, not just of him but of the avatars of love, a heresy that she squashes at once, lest she be left with the larger question of what she is planning to do with herself, why she's been placed on this earth at all. So far, he is the most plausible reason she has managed to find.

3

ON A BALMY AFTERNOON THREE WEEKS LATER, BELLE is being interviewed again, this time by an Englishman in his thirties, dressed in pinstripes, with a pale narrow face, sparse eyelashes, and a publisher's contract to write a book about Clay. His predecessors have been earnest academics, or critics eking out a meager living writing on organic space in Brancusi. Mark Dudley has two fat best-sellers to his credit, true-life crime stories about Texas millionaires murdered by their heirs. And he is armed with an agent, a gilt-edged lawyer, a paid researcher, and an option for a movie version of the book.

Lawyers' letters have been dispatched, she has declared her intention not to cooperate, but nobody seems to think that matters much. The publisher's attorney wrote a faintly menacing letter in reply: "Unfortunately, in cases like this, the first to come forward are often those with personal or professional axes to grind, which makes it even more regrettable that your point of view will not be represented." So she has finally agreed to this meeting, reduced to the humiliation of asking Dudley to wait until she is dead. And he has said, gallantly, that he hopes that won't be for a long time yet.

"You strike me as very much the sort who'll live to be ninety-three. And terrify everybody right up to the end."

"I want it on record that I don't consider you qualified to write this book."

"Yes, I've gathered that. But I may surprise you yet. At least wait until you've read it."

"I don't want to read it. Not unless I have the right to veto anything I don't like."

"I'd probably feel just the same if I were in your shoes. Would you mind if I taped this conversation? It's really for your protection, so I can't misquote you."

Grudgingly, she gives her permission, and he brings out a tiny machine from his jacket pocket, affixing a microphone to the front of her baggy dress; he pats her kindly on the shoulder before he returns to his chair.

"Let's just begin at the beginning, shall we? Tell me about the first time you met him."

"I'd rather not."

"Then you choose the subject, I'm not bothered."

"I don't want to tell you anything at all. That wasn't the deal."

He sighs. "If I may be obvious for a moment, Miss Prokoff, we're hopelessly at odds here. I'm committed to this project, and you're committed to stopping me. But I'm afraid it's not going to work, you know. Isn't there any way you can live with that?"

"Tell me why you want to write this book."

"I suppose because I'd like to read it. That's always struck me as the best possible reason for writing something."

"It's not the kind of thing you've done before. Why him?"

"Ah, that's easy. Because I have this fascination with America, you see. And he was the ultimate American painter. The quintessential American genius."

"I've never used that word. Never. Not even when I first met him. And you know damn well how I met him, you've read all about it. Haven't you?"

"Of course. But that's never the same as hearing it from someone who was actually there. You're the only eyewitness to what happened."

"Yes, and you've heard my evidence already. You think I'll tell you something I've never told before?" She snorts. "I got a two-penny postcard that said I'd been chosen for a group show uptown, and it listed everyone else who was in the show. He was the one person I hadn't heard of, so I asked around, and then I went to his apartment. Out of curiosity. And the paintings were like nothing I'd ever seen before. They knocked me out. You know all that. I stayed there, and we talked. For twelve hours. And that was that."

But she is remembering everything she's left out, a whole universe: the particular, hollow quiet of his apartment that afternoon, the pepper and egg sandwich she had eaten for lunch, the rip in his T-shirt where his belly showed through. How she had not slept the night before because her last lover had abandoned her and her painting was going nowhere and her best friend, her sole ally against the world, was preoccupied with an unworthy bearded poet. There was grit on the floor of the hallway, she could feel it crunching under her feet as she walked behind him, and grime on the windows of the room where the paintings were, with sunlight filtering through it. Had any of those things been otherwise, or if she had not been disillusioned with politics by then, and in despair over her failures, or if she had been born with high cheekbones and a sunny disposition, it might all have been different. She might have walked back down the stairs and returned to a bench in Washington Square Park to argue about Trotsky.

What she never says is that she thought she was embarking on something as simple as happiness — the very sound of his voice, with its round Western vowels, was like the promise of a world without ghosts. She was used to words being bitten off, to the clotted gutturals of her childhood, heavy with shtetl sorrow. She was used to the defensive ironies of her Village friends, children of immigrants themselves, the quick mocking laughter of people who had always known that the world was out to get them if it could. He seemed free of all that — of history, of irony. She could not imagine that he had ever been touched by ugliness, that there was anything he needed to hide.

Mark Dudley smiles encouragingly. "You probably recall exactly what you talked about, too."

"Picasso. Matisse. Whether there's such a thing as constant truths, and whether art can reveal them. It was the kind of thing people talked about in those days." Now she has told him something, after all, about what it was like back then, a particular form of religion that flourished in the mid-twentieth century. But he regards her with the same charming smile as before.

Nor does he ask her, as he should, what the work she saw that day looked like, or if any of it survived. In the whole time he has been there, he has barely glanced at her paintings, facing him on the wall; he has looked instead at her Shaker chairs, as though speculating on their value.

"And what sort of thoughts did you have when you got home that night?" Trying to catch her out, trying to see if she blushes, or says, "I didn't go home."

"About the paintings," she says, looking him in the eye. "Who else have you talked to?"

"Nobody yet. I wanted you to be the first, you see. It became rather a point of honor for me."

"Then who are you planning to talk to?"

"I'm not actually sure at the minute. I suppose it depends on the questions I find myself most concerned with."

"You're lying to me."

"Really, Miss Prokoff, that's a bit strong, isn't it? "

"Let me ask you something else."

"Certainly."

"Do you have a background in art?"

"You could have been a journalist yourself, you know. You ask all the uncomfortable questions."

"So answer me."

"I haven't had any formal training, if that's what you mean. But after reading certain of our distinguished critics I'm not really sure that's a drawback. It may even put me at a slight advantage.

It's amazing the rubbish the professionals have produced. Frankly, I think I can do better."

"Because you've got common sense?"

"Something like that. I look at what's there in the work, I don't bring a lot of theories to it."

"So you plan to start a revolution in art criticism."

"Nothing quite as grandiose as that. But I'd like to think I might reopen the field to the passionate amateur."

"That still doesn't explain why you chose him as your subject."

"I beg your pardon?"

"Answer me this. Would you be so taken with the project if he hadn't been a drunk?"

"All right, Miss Prokoff" — does she imagine it, or has his accent turned coarser? — "let's call off the dogs for a moment, shall we?" He examines his elegant hands. "You know" — in a purely conversational voice — "there are plenty of people out there who'd be delighted to tell me what they know. About the girl, for instance."

"Take this thing off me."

"With pleasure."

"And now I'm going upstairs to take a nap. Nina will see you out."

If we assume that, when she followed Clay Madden down the hall in November 1940, she was dragging her whole past behind her, then we have to begin in Odessa, in 1899, where her father joined a revolutionary cell. The meetings took place in a windowless basement that smelled of sweat, and all the members wore grimy black coats. Her father argued against violence and copied out passages from Kropotkin for distribution to the populace. Through a mere fluke — his mother was sick, he had stayed home with her that night instead of attending the meeting — he failed to be arrested with the other members, who were seized with their pamphlets and shot a few weeks later.

Soon afterwards, he was smuggled out to Bremen, and then to the New World, where he spent his life atoning for the guilt of his survival. He was busy night and day with other people's problems, teaching English to more recent immigrants, finding them jobs and housing, collecting clothes for their children; he lent them money out of his meager plasterer's earnings, joined committees, worked at settlement houses. Almost every night he could be found at some meeting of Socialist reformers, while at home, unnoticed by him, his wife was going mad and locking his children in the closet for imagined infractions. For months at a time, she fed their daughters on scraps from the garbage cans at the Pritkin Street market. Once she sold their shoes and kept them home from school, shutting the door against the visits of the truant officer. She heard voices that told her to prepare for a great disaster. She pawned her mother-in-law's wedding ring; she concealed silver dollars in socks and behind a loose brick in the chimney.

And what did all of that have to do with Clay Madden? Only that it had made Belle think she was prepared for anything, she could bear any amount of pain, when actually her innocence was as total in its way as she imagines those two girls' to have been. She had prided herself on her toughness, not knowing that one form of unhappiness in no way inured you to another, that it was possible to suffer and suffer and have it be different every time.

But she is hardly about to explain that to Mark Dudley. She is willing to talk, to the right people, about struggle, hard times, misery even, but the story has to end in triumph, vindication; there can be no suggestion of an error being made.

It's why they come to see her, after all: as much as the posthumous life of his paintings, it is the story of their life together, their dedication, their heroic sacrifice, that draws them. It restores people's faith in something large enough to battle for. And the rest — the drinking, the craziness, the car crash — becomes blurred, a matter of vague romantic legend. Somehow she is going to have to stop that man, before he can do her serious damage.

4

ALL OVER THE CITY, THEY WERE PLACING THEIR LIVERS in jeopardy — aging graduates of Pratt and Cooper Union and RISD, ex-scholarship students all, the sons of farmers and factory workers and traffic cops back in Racine. Their skin was an unhealthy gray, their hands outsized for their bodies. Having been educated for higher things, they sheetrocked for a living, or installed malachite counters and cherrywood cabinets in the kitchens of those whose luck had been better than theirs. They were men — it was different for the women, though no easier — who in a certain stage of drunkenness might take a train to Boston, or a plane to Chicago, which they could not afford, to look at a Courbet or a Seurat they had seen once and remembered lovingly for years; they were capable when they closed their eyes of tracing the exact, bosomy line of a hill in a Claude Lorraine landscape, and then of lurching from their beds to piss in the sink.

Later, they might scrape off a shape whose edge had been driving them crazy, to replace it with a better one, and stepping back think that what they had done was worth it after all; they had made something serious and beautiful. But such thoughts could only be sustained in the dead of night, when the mind reverts to its pre-post-modernist habits. During the day belief was impossible. The whole lofty enterprise was in a shambles, loftiness itself was in a shambles; Jesse Helms didn't know the half of it. In England, the fattest and richest prize went to a pair of pee-stained jockstraps; at MOMA, neon signs flashed, "Fuck and live. Suck and die," which the curator praised as Wittgensteinian. Art had become fun, had become irony, a party from which they were excluded, and they were left, clumsy and foolish, stumbling around in the Victorian dark.

So they drank for consolation, in the more grungy downtown bars, ranting against the art world, against the homosexual Mafia, the intellectual whores, against Salle and Krueger and Koons. There were too many fucking painters, they said, too many paintings; one of them had figured out, while reading the Sunday Arts and Leisure Section on the toilet, that if, as the *Times* said, there were 60,000 painters in the five boroughs, that meant a rough output of a million paintings a year. It seemed unlikely that posterity would wade through the debris to find their own. "There haven't been 60,000 painters since the beginning of time," they told each other, snorting, and started all over again, railing against the loss of rigor, of craft, all the outmoded things they had tried so righteously, so pointlessly, finally so angrily, to uphold.

Haranguing the powers that be, they saw themselves as outsiders, persecuted rebels, and yet they were reactionaries, sons of the laboring classes aligned unwittingly with the oppressor. They were protesting the decline of standards, the erosion of an ancient, elite art under attack for excluding the masses. But they were not prepared to rally behind Hilton Kramer. They were not even interested, really, in their philosophical dilemma, only the latest scrawled outrage at the Whitney ("Fuck Racism," in crayoned letters, taking up a whole wall), a Guggenheim grant to a woman who had done 7000 tracings of her vagina, the three yellow balloons that were hanging on the walls of some gallery on West Broadway, or lying on its floor. They were too busy raging, and grieving, to sort things out.

The repetitiveness of the conversation, the endless circling of the same themes, their own impotence to affect the outcome, drove them further into drunkenness. At 1:00 or 2:00 or 3:00 in the morning, they stumbled out into the street and told the beggar at the corner to fuck off, before going to the all-night Greek place for some souvlaki and taking the subway home. The next morning, badly hung over, they would show up again to nail sheetrock or paint a ceiling — they were disciplined men in their way, having learned it in their craft — or renovate the loft of an entertainment lawyer, with its obligatory Warhols over the couch, and imagine slashing them with their Stanley knives. It had come to the point where the only happy endings they could imagine centered on destruction — shooting a dealer or smashing up a loft.

This is the world that Paul Doherty occupies, though he isn't painting ceilings for a living. He is lucky enough, or compromised enough, to be teaching painting instead. Years ago, he had a tenured job at Stony Brook, but he quit in a spasm of disgust when the visiting artist program was suspended and the money went for a new carpet in the auditorium. Shortly before that, he had discovered that only one of the graduating seniors in his advanced painting class had ever been to the Met. A year later, having exhausted his savings and his options, unable even to scrape by on his sales, he became an adjunct instructor at two lesser institutions, driving his battered car to inconvenient community colleges on Long Island, where he now teaches for an hour here and an hour there. But that seems to him a minor humiliation; he never thought of himself as an assistant professor of painting.

Like the rest of them, it is the art world that is driving him mad. When he was fifteen, he used to drag his easel and his paints through the parks of Melbourne on Saturday mornings, walking miles to find the right view. At school he had been the wunderkind, the youngest person ever to be admitted to the best art college in the city; at eighteen he sent a painting to the Royal Academy, in the mother country, where it was accepted for the Summer Exhibition. At nineteen he worked his way to Le Havre as a deckhand; then he hitch-hiked to Aix-en-Provence, where he found that a housing project had been built opposite Cezanne's studio, blocking the view of Mt. Saint Victoire. At twenty-one he was awarded all the major prizes distributed to the last-year students, as well as the Governor-General's Medal in Art. At twenty-three he won a competition to paint a mural in the opera house. At twenty-five he left for New York, convinced that he could conquer that too. Now he cannot even get a show back in Australia, he has been forgotten there, and here he is, aged forty-two, stumbling from one unprofitable show to another, in galleries that serve as tax write-offs for the heirs to dry goods fortunes.

At times he still believes that he is doing something important. At times, when he looks at his paintings, or reads what others have said about his paintings, he is convinced that he has extended the boundaries enough to have mattered, at least a little, and some day that will be obvious to anyone paying attention. He spends what money he has on the kind of paint that will last forever, he prepares his canvases as they did in the old days and splurges on fine linen, all so the pigment will not fade or crack, the paintings will be ready when their time comes.

But sometimes he suspects that even to think that way is ridiculous, that the whole notion of posterity is as outdated as the code of chivalry. He might as well be dressing in armor and prancing around on a horse. And sometimes he is afraid that Clay Madden finished painting off, took it as far as it could go with those genius splatters and splashes of his. If it had all come to an end before he, Paul Doherty, even started, then his struggles are nothing but a bad joke, he is doomed to oblivion through no fault of his own. So he gets drunk again, and picks a fight, and returns to Brooklyn on the subway, glaring at the raucous Dominican teenagers opposite, who are still managing to have a good time.

He would never take Lizzie to his downtown hangouts. They are his retreat from her innocence, her solemn faith in his future, which sometimes, though he loves her for it, seems too heavy a burden to bear. He could not explain to her why he likes their dinginess and stale smells, why he likes sitting in the semi-darkness with people in worse shape than himself. More and more, except when he is seeing her, or teaching a class, he is drunk, unshaven, dirty. It is easier to feel depressed when he has not bathed, and something in him clings to his misery, is comforted by it even. It doesn't seem like an emotional state but a higher form of knowledge. At the same time he dreams, obsessively, of the day when everything will be different, when he can phone her to say he has been discovered, he is having a show someplace wonderful. On that day, his real life will begin; maybe he will even ask her to move in with him, something he wants and cannot imagine, something he hopes he will want in earnest once he has nothing left to hide.

5

"YOU'RE SURE HE HASN'T WRITTEN TO YOU?"

"Of course I'm sure," Ernest says testily. "I'm not completely senile yet."

"He's bound to approach you sooner or later."

"And what is it exactly I'm not supposed to tell him? That the will is hidden under the floorboards?"

"Don't be snide."

"I'm trying to understand what has you so alarmed. His drinking is hardly a secret to anyone at this point."

"I just didn't like that man."

"You don't like most people. You never have."

"Stop that."

"It wasn't meant as a criticism."

"I don't know why I bother telling you things . . . he's going to write a big pretentious book with all the trashy details disguised as insights. I've been reading his other ones, I've figured out his technique. He knows just how to dish out the dirt and sound superior at the same time."

"Then nobody whose opinion you could possibly care for will take it seriously."

"That's no consolation, and you know it."

"No. But it's the best I can do. Should I refuse to see him?"

"I guess not. Just try to be intimidating. And be careful what you give away."

"I don't remember very much anymore, except the work. I couldn't even say for certain how I met him."

"I could. I could say exactly."

"That's because you don't read enough."

It was at an uptown gallery, one of the few outposts of affluence in the shabby art world of those days, some time in 1942. For the past ten years the same four hundred people had been circulating and recirculating at Artists' Union dances, protests about cutbacks at the Mural Project, the parties of Mr. Guggenheim's baroness. Of those four hundred, half were painters, and one hundred and fifty of them were on the Project, though at any given moment a third might just have been laid off, to be hired back later. By the time she met Clay, Belle had danced or argued or marched with them all at one time or another. In her tight-trousers-and-red-lipstick phase, her hard-faced sorrowing period, after a White Russian sculptor had moved out of her apartment without even a note, she had slept with quite a few of them too.

But Clay had rescued her from that, at least in the beginning. Suddenly, everyone else seemed superfluous, as did argument, theory, politics, even the interminable talk about art that used to keep her from her studio for hours at a time. Her sense of amazement — at his paintings, the veins in his forearms, the stories he told her in bed of watching a herd of wild horses cross a canyon — might have lasted forever, if he had not started disappearing at night, only to bang at her door when it was just turning light, calling to her to let him in. The first time she found him swaying on the landing, she thought he must be sick, or hurt, even that someone had shot him. That was how little she knew about drunks.

By the time they met Ernest, though, fifteen months later, she had passed through many stages of knowledge. She had learned that pleading and crying and threatening to leave did not work. She had learned that reasoning with him did not work, guile did not work, and neither did rage. She had given up hiding the liquor, thrown out the homeopathic remedies and the vitamin drinks that were supposed to cure hangovers. At a certain point that winter, her head had suddenly cleared; she stopped taking things personally.

He had summoned her to look at a painting he'd had just finished; he listened to her praise with a glittering, euphoric smile on his face, but he didn't seem to hear her. And then she understood: the air in the studio was dense, for him, with more than cigarette smoke; it was crowded with ghosts — not of the dead, but of people yet to be, his future admirers. The unfamiliar smile was for his public. And she saw that, in order to get what she wanted, she would have to make the world do its part.

So she got back in touch with her old circle. With minimal resistance, he tagged along with her to openings at the galleries, the Whitney, the Modern, though he only stood in the corners, watching. She was the one who approached the reviewers and dealers and those much rarer creatures, the collectors, whom she recognized by their clothes, by the angle of their heads, their air of having better places to get to. She grew expert at ingratiating herself with them, quoting the French symbolists, expressing opinions just outrageous enough to be entertaining. In the old days, trying to bring her own work to people's notice, she had used the direct frontal assault, glaring fiercely and demanding that they come take a look. Now she acquired the diplomacy she had once scorned, a talent for flattery of a cleverly indirect kind. She was applying the degraded cunning she had learned from dealing with a drunk.

With Ernest, however, it was different.

She had not seen him for years when she and Clay walked into that gallery, but she recognized him right away. During her waitressing days at a coffee house in the Village, he had been her particular object of resentment, the only one of the regulars to treat her like a waitress and nothing else. But then he treated everyone like a waitress, or like an acolyte in need of correction, endlessly instructing the artists in his fastidious goat-like voice. Once, when he was holding forth about Picasso — "More of a draughtsman, really, than a painter; there's no real love of paint there" — she had told him, setting down his cheese sandwich, that he was full of shit, but he gave no indication that he'd heard.

And now there he was, all alone in a corner of the gallery, cocking his head at a Surrealist painting of brain matter strewn over the ocean floor. Her first impulse was to provoke him if she could.

"Hello," she said brashly, joining him, and he raised an eyebrow. "We met at the Excelsior," not mentioning that she'd been waiting on tables there.

"Ah yes." He went back to looking at the painting.

"So what are you doing these days?"

He folded his arms across his chest. "Actually," he said, elaborately casual, "I've been writing a little criticism. For the Speaker. Which is why I'm here, to find something to say about these paintings."

"And what have you found?"

He coughed. "I haven't had sufficient time with them yet."

"I know what I'd say."

"And what's that?"

"Nobody should be that self-conscious about his unconscious."

"I see."

"Don't you agree?"

"There may be an element of truth there. Are you a painter yourself?"

"Yes."

"Well, thank you for your opinion."

"I know someone whose work you should look at."

"Not yourself, I presume."

"No...but he's here." She pointed to Clay, leaning against the opposite wall. "That's him. He's going to be a great painter."

Ernest groaned. "That's a terrible thing to say about a man."

She shrugged. "Come meet him, anyway."

"What do you think of that?" Clay asked him, gesturing

towards the largest canvas in the room. A huge, glistening tendril of seaweed was coiled around the neck of a creature half-fish and half-woman, her eyes bulging out of her scaley head.

"I think the artist has read a little too much Freud and seen too much Dali."

"He hasn't seen a fucking thing. He's never looked."

Ernest seemed unaccountably pleased; he even laughed, a sort of strangled cackle in his throat. "He'd probably say he was showing us the nether regions of consciousness."

"He can say anything he wants. It doesn't make it true."

"Then shall we get out of here? I think we've looked at these long enough."

At the bar he took them to, around the corner from the gallery, a jazz trio was playing, but Ernest hardly seemed to notice. After shepherding them to a booth, he put his elbows on the table, leaned towards them, and said gleefully, over the noise, "Do you realize how much money will be pouring into New York after the war? This is going to be the center of the art world, not Paris. It's where the money is."

Belle was indignant. "It's not the money, it's the artists. All the Europeans who've come here: that's what's changing things."

"Everybody says that, but it's a lie. Why do artists get so upset when people talk about money?"

Their drinks arrived, and he was silent just long enough to sip cautiously at his Manhattan. Then he launched into what seemed to be a history of the relationship between art and money. He talked about the Medici, and Henry VIII and Holbein, and El Greco's subversive portrait of the Pope. At times Belle lost the drift entirely, especially when the saxophone was wailing, but then Ernest's voice would break through again. She caught the words "commodity fetishism" and "the secularization of the religious impulse"; she thought she heard him say that Freud had never really understood the experience of art. "Like so many systematizers, he lacked the capacity for awe." During the trumpet solo, she could make out very little, but he appeared to be tracking the rise in price of a certain Cézanne landscape over the years. When the music stopped, however, he was talking about the English, how they had never had a visual culture. Maybe it was their weather, he said, shaking his head regretfully, or their famous lack of sensuality. "Think of their cooking." He rolled his eyes. "Literature is the enemy of art. Take away Turner, and all their so-called art is merely illustration."

Clay, who had only nodded and frowned throughout, crossing and uncrossing his legs where they sprawled in the aisle, asked suddenly, "So what do you think of Ryder?"

"Why do you ask?"

"Because I want to know."

Ernest sighed. "He's a difficult one, isn't he? An eccentric. Not part of the grand procession, not a major influence. But still . . ."

"Still what?"

"I'd never dismiss him. He saw something of his own. There's a genuine struggle there."

"You're a good man," Clay said. "You want to come see my paintings?"

"Certainly."

He paid for the drinks, brushing aside their money, and a few minutes later they were on the subway, headed downtown. Even Picasso, Ernest told them over the screech of the train, had not fully absorbed the implications of relativity. An ancient, skinny drunk got on and sat down next to him, falling asleep with his grimy head bobbing onto Ernest's shoulder. Each time Ernest tried to move away, the old man slumped down further, until his head found the shoulder again. Finally Clay stood up and propped him firmly against the back of the seat. "So that's what one does," Ernest said, with interest.

They marched up the five flights of stairs in single file, Clay in the lead. When Clay switched on the lights in the studio, Ernest bounded into the room, blinked, and came to a halt. He moved slowly from painting to painting, silent at last, his nostrils flared slightly.

Meanwhile Clay followed him warily with his eyes; it was apparent that he had accepted Ernest at his own evaluation. Belle had not been sure up till then whether to regard him as a joke or a prophet; now she too watched him anxiously, awaiting his verdict. Ernest pursed his lips and went around the room again.

"Let me put it like this," he said finally. "At the moment, your ambition outstrips your authority. Reach exceeding grasp, and all that. But . . ." He paused. "There's something here, there's no doubt about that. You're finding your own way into the interior."

"But did I get there yet?"

"Are you serious?"

"I don't know. Maybe."

Ernest shook his head and returned to the first painting. "You should change this green here, it's muddy," he said. "You might want to try a blue . . . or maybe, no, a brown. Go for the real mud and see what happens."

"That's not what I asked."

"No one can say how you should paint your paintings before they exist. But once they're here they can be taken farther. There are limits to the virtues of spontaneity. You should listen to me, because I'll certainly come here again."

"And then what?"

"What do you mean?"

"Then what happens?"

"How the hell should I know?"

After that, improbably, they were allies. The very things that Clay found suspect in other people — especially other painters — were matters to boast about in Ernest; for the next fifteen years, she would have to put up with his pride in Ernest's learning. "You're the one that does the paintings, he can only talk about them," she told him, but a minute later he was describing to someone how Ernest read philosophy at the breakfast table: "I swear to God, I've seen him do it," he'd say, as if it was too astonishing for anyone to believe. Sometimes he tried reading it himself, but after a page of Ernest's beloved Hegel he got up and stared out the window; resolutely, he started over, only to shut the book a little later and sit there scowling, wounded by his own failure, or disappointed, maybe, that he had not found the enlightenment he sought.

Ernest, meanwhile, though he might proclaim to the world that Clay was a great painter, showed no such reverence in his dealings with him. That, too, fueled her resentment for years, right up till Clay's death, when the general reverence became so great, and numbing, that she seemed in danger of being subsumed. It was then that she finally started to love Ernest.

6

JUST AS BELLE THOUGHT, MARK DUDLEY HAD LIED when he told her she was the first person he'd spoken to. By the time he appeared at her door that day he had already tracked down several people who knew them when they lived in the Village, a man who had worked with her at the WPA, a nurse who took care of Clay in the mental hospital he'd been in right before he met Belle. There were also two old men who knew her at the Academy of Design, and a suburban grandmother who was in the one class Clay took at the Art Students League. Mark Dudley has recorded all those people, their ramblings and reminiscences, filled for the most part with irrelevancies ("She chewed a lot of gum, I remember that much"; "He never spoke a word to me the whole term") and had the tapes transcribed by a secretarial service. Meanwhile, the assistant his researcher has found in Montana is hunting up people who knew Clay's family when he was a child. As soon as her list is complete, he will fly out there.

He has also located Belle's sister, in Brooklyn, which none of his predecessors ever did, and entered her address and phone number on his computer; before approaching her, though, he needs to see how things will develop with Belle. For the same reason, he hasn't yet tried to talk to any of the people who knew them out on the Island; he's not about to blow his chances with her for the sake of a handyman's evidence.

But his greatest coup has been Sophie Horowitz, Belle's best friend in her Village days. "It was like we were in love, I mean it. It was a real schoolgirl romance we had going, only we were twenty-three." The two women have not spoken in almost forty years. "Because of him, of course. Because I couldn't stand the way he treated her, it made me sick, and I told her so." She looked at him defiantly, a tiny bent woman in a wheelchair who seemed for a moment, from the very force of her vehemence, to be rising, or swelling, out of it.

"It wasn't love, it was thrall. Thrall. Like in the fairy tales. And she'd always been the one to tell the rest of us not to do that, to get on with our own painting and not throw everything away for some man. She was so fierce back then, I wish you could have known her. But he was a genius, she said, that made it different, only it came down to the same thing. You wouldn't believe how women were in those days; you can't even imagine it. Our parents came to America to give us a better life, and the boys had a better life, but the girls, they had the same life as always. She had her mother's life, that she hated; her mother was married to a great man, a big person, she was just the servant, and that's what she did too. It's almost funny. A good course in Freud might have saved her, only she didn't believe in Freud, she believed in art. Don't get me started on that one."

But of course getting her started was exactly what he was there to do. That first day, however, she would not talk any more about Belle, no matter how he tried to lead her. She talked about politics instead, about the decline of the left, starting with the 60s rebels and their childish antics, the ongoing cowardice of the Democrats. The second time, too, she dangled her knowledge in his face and then pulled back, understanding full well that once she had told him all she knew he might never come back. He is used to such interviews, to talking to lonely old people with secrets to be meted out. It is part of his job, which he is good at.

Already he has visited her three times in the nursing home in

Ardsley, a converted millionaire's mansion where she spends her days sitting in her wheelchair on the white veranda, dressed in a hot pink track suit. All the others, too, strapped into their chairs, slumped over and staring into space, are dressed for jogging, but unlike them, she does not mutter or moan to herself. She seems to be the only inmate with her mental faculties intact. "Landscape," she says, gesturing at the golf course a hundred yards away, where a weeping willow stirs in the breeze. "Sometimes it's a Ruysdael, sometimes it's a Constable, sometimes it's just a Hopper. More and more it's a Hopper. I'm losing my sense of splendor. Don't ever get old, Mr. Dudley."

"I wish you'd call me Mark."

"Mark, then. Have you been to see her yet?"

"Not yet."

"They say she's got terrible arthritis — she used to be a wonderful dancer, did you know that? She'd go to all the dances and drag some man out onto the floor just so she could show off. I used to love to watch her. Of course he didn't dance at all; she must have given it up when she met him. Along with everything else."

"Was that what your fight was about?"

"We had lots of fights. I yelled at her, I pleaded with her, I did everything but get down on my knees. She used to write him these letters — you know the kind, the ones women write to men who are making them miserable. They were living together, but she'd write him these letters and leave them for him on the kitchen table. 'We can't go on like this,' stuff like that. Analyzing his problems, and her problems, and their problems. Sometimes she'd bring them over to my place and read them to me. They could break your heart, those letters, they were so reasonable, she was trying so hard to understand, to sort everything out. And then he'd read them and say, 'You're right,' only nothing changed."

"So you advised her to stop writing letters?"

"Why should I do that? That wasn't the point, the letters. The point was she should have left him. She used to keep a journal, too, where she'd write it all down, everything that was going on, in these little notebooks like the schoolchildren used. Maybe it helped her. She wasn't painting much in those days. And then one day he found one, and I guess he threw some kind of almighty shit fit. After that she'd hide them at my place. She made me promise not to read them, either."

"And did you?"

"I wouldn't do that behind her back. Not then. She made me put them in a special place so that Howard wouldn't find them — my husband, only he wasn't my husband then. Howard Aronow. The poet. I'd put them in my underwear drawer and places like that. These little black notebooks with speckles on the front."

"What did your husband think of Clay Madden?"

"He hardly ever saw him. Howard was in Washington during the war, working for the Writers' Project in some mansion down there, and it was during the war that she and I stopped being friends. Or no — right after the war. Peace had been declared, and then we had our last fight. The really big one."

"But you'd had the same fight before?"

"Not quite like that."

"What was different about it?"

"It was about the Jews. I don't want to talk about it."

"You wouldn't by any chance still happen to have any of those notebooks, would you?"

"I might. So what do you think about our elections? You think the goddamn Republicans are going to pull it off?"

Sophie was being difficult again, was watching her in that accusatory way, passing judgment, or rather confirming the various judgments she had already passed. For months now it had been going on like that. She hardly even seemed to talk any more; she merely watched and waited, until it was time to pounce. And Belle, who had always been more completely herself with Sophie than with anyone else, kept jabbering on evasively about things she no longer even thought about: her job at the WPA, for example, which had been cut back to half-time, and her boss, who was driving her mad, she said, which wasn't remotely true, because she forgot his existence the minute she stepped outside.

This time she found herself trying to entertain Sophie with stories about her piecework, as she called it, which consisted of painting horses on ties. The man who paid her had been complaining lately about the quality of her tails: "You haven't captured the poetry for me," he said. But Sophie was not amused. Her face was a pantomime of reproach; she fidgeted in her chair, quivering with the need to get it out.

"Why doesn't he paint the horses?" she asked, meaning Clay. "Then you'd have some time for your painting."

"Did you just want to see me so you could do this?"

"Do what?"

"What you're doing now."

"I'm worried about you, that's all."

"Well, don't be."

"You haven't even mentioned the war. I bet you never give it a thought." Sophie bit her lip. "You're like someone pushing a piano up a flight of stairs."

"What's that supposed to mean?"

"I don't know. Just an image that came to me. You'll never admit you're in trouble."

"For Christ's sake, Sophie."

"You're in a bad way, you know that? Like someone under a spell."

"Can't you let up for five minutes?"

For a second they glared at each other. Then Sophie ducked her head and traced a figure eight on the marble tabletop. "So Madame Dreyfus is going to give him a show uptown. That's great."

"It is, sort of."

"What about your painting? What's happening with that?"

Belle set down her cup. "Could you not start on that one?"

"You're burying yourself alive for him."

"I'm not."

"Of course you are. And you're the one who used to yell about that louder than anyone."

"It's not personal. It has nothing to do with the personal. It's about something else."

"That's bullshit."

"It isn't. You saw his paintings. You know how good they are."

"I don't know. I thought some of your stuff last year was pretty good."

"Don't be ridiculous. Not like that."

"So you've dedicated yourself to his genius."

"I am not some poor girlie fresh out of art school. I know what I'm doing. What time is it?"

"Ten past six."

"I've got to go." She stood up. "Our presence is required at Rosie's tonight, and I have to iron my black dress. Are you going to give me flak about that too?"

"You're just angry because you know I'm right. Because I want you to be a serious person." Sophie sighed, a *yenta's* sigh, full of ostentatious patience. "Forget it. I'll walk you to the corner."

They both dropped some coins on the table and gathered up their things. "I don't know," Belle said. "Who the hell knows what's going on?" They both knew it was a kind of peace-offering, however lame; she was saying she did not want Sophie to give up on her yet.

They were almost to the corner where they would part when Sophie spoke again. "So is she really as crazy as they say?"

"Who?"

"You know. La Dreyfus."

Belle slowed down, considering. "Sometimes I think she's no crazier than the rest of us, she just never had to learn to control herself. So it's all right out there, the stuff that everyone else hides."

"But you spend time with her, you go to her parties. Do you like her?"

"Once in a while I feel sorry for her. Nobody could like her."

"Well, that's a relief."

"Why?"

"Because, *honeleh*, you start liking people like Rosie Dreyfus, you're really done for. *Geendicht*. There's only so much money a person can have in this world and not turn evil. She's got a lot more than that."

7

HER FULL NAME WAS ROSALIND—ROSALIND FLEISCH-
mann Dreyfus — and she was the real thing, a Medici, an heiress,
with a mane of frizzy red hair and the galloping lusts of a feudal
baron. She had had forty-three years to learn that no one would
ever love her for herself alone; most of the time she seemed like the
perfect predator, all will and appetite and scarlet lipstick, but in
unguarded moments her face could take on the desolate look of a
woman in a Walker Evans photograph.

Things might have gone better for her if she had stuck to the
company of the very rich, who would certainly have welcomed her
despite her bad table manners and the dirty slip that always
showed beneath her hem. She could have sailed the Aegean on
their yachts, sat with them at the best tables in the best restaurants,
her lips gleaming with animal fat, avidly crunching up bones with
her sharp teeth. But her cravings were all for art, for the life of the
spirit, which she somehow thought she could achieve by taking
artists to bed. And then, of course, things always deteriorated fast.
Between what she wanted, which was something like redemption,
and what they wanted, which was much more basic than that,
there could be no reconciliation.

It was on realizing this that, inevitably, she sought revenge.
Her bloodlines on both sides were full of robber barons, men who
had specialized in the destruction of their enemies, and this spirit

still lived in her, though she lacked their ruthless self-control. She shrieked and howled, threw heavy objects from windows, slashed the canvases she had paid good money for. It was said that, like Ibsen's heroine, she had once burned the only manuscript of an indigent writer's novel, after finding him naked with another woman in the house she had lent him in the south of France.

In the last months before the war, she had raced around Paris buying up paintings cheap from their panic-stricken makers. La Vautoure, the artists called her — the vulture — as she bullied them into parting with their best canvases. But when she sailed for America on the S.S. *France*, she brought with her not only their paintings but some of them, too, the ones in most danger from the Nazis — three Communists and three Jews, several with wives and children — for whom she had miraculously, with the help of heavy bribes, obtained visas. Back in New York, she installed all thirteen of her new dependents in a townhouse near the East River that she had bought years before and never lived in because she disliked the staircase. She brought them oxtails and brown bread and oil crayons, hired a little man to tutor them in English, but like all the previous objects of her generosity, they showed no signs of gratitude. The crayons were the wrong brand, the light was hopeless to work in, she had never told them they would all be sharing a kitchen. Fights broke out among the women, who demanded that she referee. One of the Communists, when she tried to seduce him, locked himself in his upstairs bedroom, threatening to leave by the window.

A few months later, they dispersed, finding themselves hole-in-the-wall apartments of their own, borrowing shamelessly from her when the rent came due. She was left with her crates full of paintings. Then, with the war on in Europe and retreat to her villa in Nice impossible, she had her inspiration: to open a gallery in New York where she could show the refugees' work. Soon they were all grumbling about her commission and the way her shows were hung. And when she announced that she was looking for American painters too, the downtown artists, though they all schemed to get her to their studios, sat around the bars mocking her pretensions to culture as well as her sexual habits. What they really minded was that she insisted on being seduced in their dingy walk-ups, rather than in her bedroom on Fifth Avenue; she believed, as they never could, in the purity of their squalor.

At last, having promised shows to far too many painters, she decided to extricate herself through a juried competition. It was there that Hugo Klesmer, the emigré painter she feared and honored most, had made a rare impassioned speech in praise of Clay's work. At first she protested — she thought he must be joking — but soon she was parroting his remarks to everyone else: "the most original painting in the room," "the first truly American art."

Thus were Clay and Belle swept into Rosie Dreyfus' orbit, or at least her outer circle, where they stood, incongruously, looking on. Belle, to whom Rosie had taken an instant dislike, was summoned to the gallery several times to help address invitations, and then shouted at for bad penmanship; once Rosie even demanded two cents for an envelope she claimed Belle had ruined. Clay, on the other hand, though he was edgy and silent around her, she treated with elaborate respect, calling him Mr. Madden in her tenderest, most girlish voice and apologizing fulsomely for every demand on his time. It was Belle who received the instructions about keeping him sober at Rosie's parties — Rosie had a whole network of informers — just as it was Belle who was expected to deliver his paintings. And Rosie invited them only to her more respectable gatherings, attended by her Park Avenue friends. For some reason, they were kept away from the parties she was famous for, where jazz musicians and actresses and Italian countesses smoked hashish in the bathroom.

When they arrived at her apartment, the night that Sophie warned Belle against her, the Europeans were clustered at the mantelpiece, with Klesmer, pale and severe, in their center. Meanwhile, the small contingent of downtown painters stayed near the bar, gulping down whiskey. Belle stuck by Clay's side, both of them sipping seltzer out of crystal tumblers, until the Blodgetts, a couple they had met at another of Rosie's parties, came over and greeted them. Mr. Blodgett, a lawyer, was large and pink-cheeked and jovial in an awkward kind of way; Mrs. Blodgett was fragile and sad and painted watercolors. She began telling Clay in her whispery voice about seeing the Marin show: "It made me want to run away to the seaside. Have you ever painted the ocean, Mr. Madden? Don't you think everyone should?" He looked tense but manful, bending down awkwardly to hear her better.

"That was a damn fine show," he said, and then fell silent. Belle started talking rapidly about the sea, quoting Conrad and Walt Whitman. She was becoming very adept with quotations. She also offered the information that Clay was a great admirer of Melville, since he'd neglected to mention that himself.

A jowly, leathery woman with bright red lipstick and a diamond pin came and greeted Mr. Blodgett, who agreed with her that the Reds seemed to be giving it to the Germans at Stalingrad. Rosie appeared, nestling against a blond boy with bad skin. "This is Anthony. He doesn't hate me as much as the rest of you."

There was a sudden blast of alto sax: somebody had turned the gramophone up. Abruptly, a few people sprang to life and started dancing. One young painter deserted the bar and started to jitterbug all by himself.

"Anthony's going to help me in the gallery," Rosie told them sweetly when the record ended. "But first we're going to spend some time cataloguing my collection."

"We've told our friend from Owens Merrill all about your paintings," Mrs. Blodgett said. "He's dying to see them."

"Send him round," Rosie said. "I love watching people fall in love with my paintings. Even Joyce admired them, although of course he can't see too well. Only the Nazis refused to be converted. At first I thought it was my Jewish parents they minded, but no, it was my decadent paintings."

"Interesting, isn't it, how seriously the Germans take art these days." It was a portly, wall-eyed little man who had been standing nearby, the center of yet another group. "But of course what most people fail to understand is that Nazism is essentially an aesthetic phenomenon."

"How brilliant," Rosie said. "What do you mean, exactly?"

He strolled over, looking pleased. "It's obvious once you think about it. Nazism is simply the Greek ideal filtered through the distorting lens of Nietzsche. The blond beast, beyond good and evil, all that relentless drive towards purity. I'm thinking of writing something on the subject."

"That's Alfred Lehrman," the leathery woman said. "He's a famous scholar, he's just written a book about Courbet." Mrs. Blodgett whispered to Clay, "Don't men like that always make you feel so shy?"

Everyone was respectfully silent, until Hugo Klesmer detached himself from the group at the fireplace. "If you had seen the ruins of Rotterdam, my friend, I do not think you would talk about aesthetics in that way."

"But that just bears out my thesis: Rotterdam is precisely what happens when one attempts to live by one's aesthetic creed. The Nazis seem mad to us because they have put into practice a theory that others have only talked about."

"That's absolutely true," Rosie said. "Professor Lehrman, you're a genius. Anthony, get me another drink."

Lehrman smiled graciously at Klesmer. "I'm not defending them, you know. It's just that I find the phenomenon interesting. You don't, I take it."

"In a hundred years, it may be acceptable to call them interesting," Klesmer said. "But not at this time, no."

Lehrman shrugged, palms in the air. "If one has been trained not to take things personally, anything can be interesting. Particularly questions related to aesthetics." Several people murmured approvingly.

"You think you'd be standing around in Germany right now talking about aesthetics?" It was Clay.

Lehrman stroked his chin, as charming as ever. "That hardly seems relevant. An observation can be true in any context."

"You're a Jew, aren't you? Your people are disappearing every day. You think they'd care about your fine distinctions?"

Rosie gave Belle a furious look, as though this must be her fault. Lehrman threw up his hands. "My dear sir, I can hardly presume to speak for any group of people. One's thoughts still belong to oneself, even in wartime."

A doggy-looking woman with a bowl haircut who had come up behind Lehrman took his arm protectively. "Why aren't you in the army," she asked Clay, "if you feel like that?"

He took a step towards her. "Because they wouldn't take me."

"Why not? You look healthy enough to me."

"That's none of your business," Belle snapped.

"Oh God," — it was Rosie — "this is ridiculous," and then to Clay, "I think you owe the professor an apology."

"No, no, that won't be necessary," Lehrman said. "It was only a misunderstanding. A quibble over art."

He had turned away when Clay yelled at his back, "You prick. You wouldn't know art if it weighed four hundred pounds and sat on your face."

For some reason Belle thought of Sophie. Everyone edged away, moving as one body, until she and Clay were marooned together in the center of the room.

And then Klesmer appeared. "How do you do?" he said briskly. Clay remained mute. "I have hoped to make your acquaintance since I saw your work." Klesmer clucked his tongue. "I cannot do all the talking. Somebody must help me. You, then," he said to Belle. She gaped at him. "We will discuss the charms of New York."

"You're being sarcastic, right? You don't really think it has any charms."

"Not at all. I think it an ideal city, except for the trees. And the museums are too crowded. If I were in charge, I would impose a large entrance fee to discourage people."

"But that's so undemocratic."

"Precisely." He beamed at her.

Now Clay was looking longingly at the door; Klesmer made a face. "You are tormenting yourself needlessly, I promise you," he said, as a dance tune came out of the gramophone. "Artists have said worse things."

"He's right," Belle said. "I don't care. Let's dance." But Clay ignored her.

"Perhaps the young lady will dance with me," Klesmer said. "And you go talk to Stefan Probst. He also admires your work. Remind him that he mustn't leave without taking his umbrella."

She could not conceive of his dancing, except in some stately eighteenth-century way, a minuet maybe; she could imagine him marching, or clicking his heels at attention, but never, ever doing the jitterbug. But that was what he proceeded to do, flinging her outward and snapping her back, his torso erect, his bony face as severe as ever, his feet, in their narrow black shoes, kicking rhythmically. When she stumbled against him, dizzy from being whirled around, she could feel the brittle bones in his chest.

Then the record ended, and he wiped his brow with a spotted handkerchief he took from his breast pocket. "When I was in Paris and would listen to such music, I used to imagine that all Americans were afficionados of *le jazz*. It was one of my greatest shocks on coming to this country, to find that so many had no knowledge of it." He replaced the handkerchief as boogie-woogie poured from the gramophone again. "Shall we try once more?"

So they did, and this time she found her rhythm; she shimmied and dipped, the mass to his line, the horizontal to his vertical; her shoulders, her arms, her pelvis were suddenly independent of her feet, could take off in whole different directions. It seemed with every passage as though she might not come back to him in time, but miraculously she always did; they were a symmetry, or more than that, a conspiracy, in league against the others, who looked on disapprovingly while they danced themselves out of reach, playing off the music, moving against it, ahead of it, until they had found their freedom.

Then he bowed to her gravely, as though they'd been dancing a minuet after all, and they started all over again.

Thirty years later, when Klesmer was long dead, she went to the opening of his retrospective at MOMA — one of the very rare occasions, by then, when she entered a museum in a spirit of homage — to be greeted by the sight of a red, medieval-style banner with a quotation from him: "All painting is about rhythm." For a minute, as she stood there in her heavy silk suit, with heavy Mexican silver around her neck, lightness descended; even her joints felt weightless, as if some other, more ethereal body were inhabiting her own. And she thought how strange it was that Klesmer, severe and ascetic Klesmer, with his thinning hair and concave chest, had managed what no one else in the world ever had; he had shown her what it felt like to be beautiful.

8

At Milo's Bar, on Lafayette Street, the subject is not the art world for a change but women. Two of the artists' girlfriends have been clamoring for babies; one of them, staring forty in the face, has moved out, taking her pots and pans with her, to look for a man who wants a family. The other is still hopeful that she can prevail; all week she has been arguing and pleading and acting sweetly reasonable, and then waking him up in floods of tears.

"You think you've finally met one who really means it, she's so independent she won't even make you a fucking cup of coffee the first night you stay over, and you think, fine, great, at least this one won't be after me about babies. But in the end it always comes back to that."

"When did you figure that out? Tonight?"

"Thirty-seven; that's when it starts creeping up on them."

"It's hard on her, I know that. Her sister just had a kid, her girlfriends all have kids. But why didn't she tell me five years ago that was what she wanted?"

"They can't help it, they've got ten thousand years of instinct programmed into their psyches. The propagation of the species. Feather the nest, find someone to dig the worms."

"Fuck the worms. I don't want to be told I've ruined someone's life. I'd never say that to anyone. I can ruin my own goddamn life, I don't need any help."

"They don't know what they want any more. They're all mixed up from this feminism shit."

"They never knew what they wanted. Even Freud said that."

"He couldn't figure it out either."

"So what are you going to do? Become a fag?"

"I'm considering it."

But what they vent to each other is always the anger; the other part, the sadness, they can only confess to women — it's what they need them for, more almost than sex. The artist whose girlfriend has moved out had his own fantasies of fatherhood; there were days when he caught himself staring at babies in the subway, the same as she did, imagining himself in a house like the one he grew up in, back in Michigan, with his children running up and down the stairs.

"What the fuck is this precious freedom of yours except the freedom to be miserable?" his girlfriend said to him as she crammed her sweaters into the matching luggage her mother had sent her for Christmas. "Do you really think you'd feel any worse if we had a kid?"

"I just can't do it," he said. "I can't change my life like that, I'm too old. If I did it I'd want to do it right, protect and provide and the whole bit. I wouldn't want my kids growing up in this slum." Really he was scared that his sense of defeat was permanent, that he could not dredge up, ever again, enough faith or hope or love of life or whatever it took to do this thing. The bartender, who used to paint himself, twenty years ago, and now has two kids out in Queens, gives him a free drink.

Meanwhile, Paul Doherty, who has sometimes vaguely imagined that if his art career took off he might have a few kids himself and teach them all to paint, is making reckless splashes on a canvas he fully intends to destroy the next day. It's not really his painting, but a pure act of homage, or of celebration; for the same reason, he is drinking as he works, neat Scotch, though he is also listening to the *Niebelungenlied*, which has nothing to do with Clay Madden.

Three hours ago he got a breathless phone call from Lizzie.

"You'll never guess where I'll be living this summer."

"In London," he said, remembering her professor.

"No. I'm going to be at Belle Prokoff's house."

"What are you talking about?"

"There was an ad posted at the Student Employment Office, she wanted a kind of companion for the summer, so I phoned her. And she remembered me! I'm starting on June 1st . . . isn't that wonderful?"

"Hang on a minute. Is it wonderful? She's supposed to be a real ball-breaker."

"I thought you'd be excited. Don't you even want to meet her?"

"Sure I do. But I can't see why you'd want to spend your summer looking after an old woman."

"Because I loved her, that's why. When I phoned her she said, 'Of course I remember you. You'll do fine.' I loved the way she said 'Of course' like that, in this very sharp voice. She's got no patience, that's what's wonderful about her."

"Just what everyone wants in an employer. What happens if she gets really ill? Do you start carrying bedpans?"

"Don't be silly. She's got arthritis, that's all."

"How do you know? Have you seen the doctor's report? Anyway, it's not the greatest thing to have on your c.v.: Nurse-companion to art widow. What about your professor?"

"I just realized I've never liked Carlyle, I don't even like Mrs. Carlyle. And I don't want to spend my whole summer in a library. I've been in a library all winter."

"That's not why you're doing it," he said, and then stopped.

"What do you mean?"

"Nothing. Never mind." He'd been going to say, "You're doing it because of me," but decided against it. It seemed risky, incriminating somehow, to say it out loud; it would make him responsible. The truth was, he wanted her to do it: he wanted to drive her and her belongings out there, on the perfect pretext that she could not carry everything on the train; he wanted to meet the widow himself. Most of all, he wanted to go into the studio and stand where Madden had done those paintings. But first he had to make some honorable effort to dissuade her.

"Just think it over, okay? Think about being stuck in the house with her for twenty-four hours a day. And then we can talk about it later."

Now he turns the music up louder. Bellowing along in his nonexistent German, he dumps some more whiskey into his glass and steps back. The painting is shit, just like the pseudo-Maddens his students turn out in droves. "Fuck it," he says, and turns off the music on his way to the phone.

"Okay. I've been thinking about this job of yours, and you're right. It's wonderful. You're wonderful. Why don't you come over here right now so I can ravish you?"

"Have you been drinking?"

"I'm not pissed, if that's what you mean. I've been painting, a godawful painting, and the fumes have probably got to me. It's dangerous stuff, paint, it can kill you. All that lead."

"You always say that . . . you know I can't take the subway out there at this hour."

"Shit. No, you can't. Take a cab. I'll pay for it."

"Why don't you come here?" It is a minor bone of contention between them that he will never spend the night at her place, with her roommates eyeing him accusingly when he arrives and running in and out of the bathroom in the morning. It makes him feel like a dirty old man, he has explained all that, but it hurts her feelings nonetheless.

"You come here instead. Go on, get a cab."

In the end she agrees, as he knew she would. He washes out his glass, he puts the Scotch away and goes to check on his sheets, to see if they are reasonably clean; in his makeshift kitchen, he washes the paint off his hands and brushes his teeth, and then, as an afterthought, his hair, the same dirty-blond color as hers. He even tends to his beard, dragging a comb through its frizzy snarls.

She has never tried to get anything from him, never blamed him, nagged him, kept a balance sheet of who did what, and now she is making him a love offering, however she denies it. He knows from experience what happens when a woman sacrifices herself for him; it always ends in disaster, but right now he wants to make her some offering in return. And so he decides to draw her; in bed that night, after they've made love, he will get out his battered sketch-book and his charcoals and draw her naked, in all her ripply-haired, oval-faced, pre-Raphaelite splendor, and give it to her.

It's been years since he's drawn anyone, except in the class-room to demonstrate a point to his students. In the late twentieth century, rendering the body seems as relevant as painting a cottage with a thatched roof. But sometimes he thinks of it with a kind of a guilty longing, as if it were a sensual pleasure forbidden him by the vows of abstraction. Now it seems like the perfect gesture, as fool-ishly romantic as picking her flowers in a meadow, though she will not understand that.

She will look at it and say, as women always did, "I look so fat," or "Is my nose really that wide?" "Are my breasts really that funny shape?" She will be hurt that he did not make her as beauti-ful as she wants to be. But some day when the children she's left him to have are squabbling and shrieking, when there are frown lines in her forehead and her respectable husband has taken to flirt-ing with younger women at dinner parties, she will take out the drawing and remember making love in his dirty loft. Then maybe she'll forgive him for whatever hurt he's going to inflict on her before they're done. She will see the way he drew her breasts, and her lips, and the light fuzz of hair between her legs, and know that he would have kept her if he could.

9

IT'S EXACTLY AS SOPHIE DESCRIBED IT TO HIM: A child's cheap exercise book, with a speckled cover and rough lined paper inside. The paper has darkened and the ink has faded, a bad combination, but the script is large and strong, the words are still clear on the page.

September 16th

Today is my father's *yortsayt*. All day I felt the shadow of him, not my sadness but his. It always hung in the air around him. And then Clay didn't come home tonight — he said he would, I told him what day it was — and the shadow was stronger than ever. But disapproving this time, because he was that, too, that was his other side. That scary-calm look he had when I had been bad: "What's going to become of you?" he'd say, with that cold look on his face. And now this has become of me. I spend my nights waiting for a drunk to come home. I march up and down the hall for hours, listening, making speeches in my head. Such blistering speeches, but still rational, Father. You'd be proud of how logical my arguments are, you'd see I learned something from you after all.

I wonder if things would be different if you were alive. I don't think I could stand to have you see me living like this. I'd be too ashamed. Maybe you'd have come and taken me away. I think that was what I always wanted, for you to rescue me, but it was always the others you rescued, the widows and orphans and the man whose legs had been crushed when he fell from a rotten bit of scaffolding. Never me.

October 4th

Tonight when Clay didn't come back I went into the kitchen and looked at his razor. I touched the edge to make sure it was sharp. Then I remembered you're supposed to do it in water, it works faster that way. So I ran a bath, and started taking off my clothes. I knew I didn't really want to die. What I wanted was to time it just right, so he would come home and find me. So finally he'd see what he was doing to me.

I'm always saying I'm going to leave him. I think we even believe that I'll do it — me as much as him. He looks so worried when I say it, all my anger goes away. Then I go make coffee, or I remind him to check in at the Project office and see if they're taking people back on this week, and we both know I'm not leaving, not yet.

October 29th

Ever since Pearl Harbor I've been worrying about the army taking him. Now it turns out there's nothing to be afraid of. He told me this morning that two years ago he spent three months in a clinic here in the city, not just a drying-out place but a real mental asylum. His own brother committed him when he came to New York on a visit.

It all came out because I told him things couldn't go on the way they are. Every night this week he's come in drunk and crazy. Last night he came and shook me awake at three in the morning to say he didn't want to live in a body any more. He stood there rocking back and forth and told me in this very slow, trance-like voice that he was going to get rid of his body, he was going to take it somewhere at night and dump it. So this morning I told him he had to get help, and then he told me. When the draft board called him in, the whole thing came out, they wrote away for his records, so he knows they won't take him. I asked him why he'd never told me, and he said, "I'm telling you now."

November 19th

For weeks the drinking has been getting worse. Last night the police picked him up for throwing a rock through Andrew Danforth's window. I couldn't exactly tell the cops that every painter in the Village wants to throw a rock at Andrew Danforth, nobody can stand the way he patronizes them. Only Clay got drunk enough to do it.

Clay said he was lecturing everyone about Surrealism, like it was his own invention. He kept going on about how much courage it takes to go deep into your unconscious. So Clay left and went to some bar on Fourteenth Street, but later he went and threw stones at Danforth's building and told him to come the hell out, he'd tell him a few things about the unconscious. And Danforth called the police. Which just shows what he's like, if we needed more proof. In his head he's still at prep school, only his tie has paint spots on it now.

It wouldn't seem like such a big deal, except when I went to the police station this morning, to bail Clay out, he was still sounding like he was drunk — screaming at the guy on duty that he'd hear about him some day, he was going to be famous. The cop couldn't even be bothered to answer. He just winked at me and rolled his eyes. I didn't think I even cared until later, when I was heading to Klein's to do the first aid windows, and I realized I had my head down so I wouldn't have to look straight at anyone, I couldn't look anyone in the eye.

The only people I could stand to look at were the bums around the fire in the lot on Twelfth Street. They didn't seem foreign any more, or scary. They finally looked exactly like everyone else to me.

When I told Clay that, he said, "You mean you never thought you could wind up like them? I feel like I've been one step away ever since I came to New York. You think no one who could paint pictures ever found himself sleeping under the el? They might have a talent, too."

November 28th

At three in the morning, it always feels as though nobody's awake but you, there's nobody out there to hear you, least of all some bearded God listening to your prayers. And you know that nothing is ever going to change, and all the worst thoughts you've ever had are true.

Last night I knew for sure it was going to go on like this forever, it was only going to get worse, not better, and that would be it, that would be our life. And I kept thinking, why us, why us, until finally I thought, Why not us? Then I got up and made some coffee and went into the studio. And I realized that I was never going to leave those paintings. I might never be sane, not really, and I probably won't ever be really happy either. But that's okay. I'll settle for the paintings.

"Would you allow me to copy some of this, Miss Horowitz? Mrs. Aronow? I wouldn't take it away with me, just copy it here."

Of course there is no question of including it all — that would require the old cow's permission — but he can quote judiciously, the lawyers will tell him just how far the fair use doctrine can be stretched. And he can paraphrase the rest. He imagines the triumphant words on the book jacket: Access to intimate diaries never before seen . . . The true story of a tormented love.

"I can't let you do that. I just wanted you to see what he did to her."

"I can assure you, I wouldn't abuse your trust."

"It wasn't like they say, it wasn't just the drinking. He was a sick man. There was one time I went to visit them on the Island during the war, with Ernest Reichinger. They'd moved out there because it was supposed to stop him drinking, but I could see things were worse than ever. He kept needling her about her work, telling her she should show it to Reichinger, when you could see she was feeling really lousy about how it was going. 'At least let Sophie see it,' he said, 'she'll like anything you do.' It was the cruelest thing I ever saw, him with this smirk on his face, and she was just cringing the whole time. Like a dog. I hated to leave her there, that was one of the worst things I ever did. Afterwards I thought, why didn't I get her out, I should have taken her with me back to the city, but it never even occurred to me at the time."

"Did you talk to her about it?"

"Not then. Not that weekend. It was like we were all paralyzed, even Reichinger. We just watched him. But later I did."

"And what did she say?"

"She said she was learning to paint, she was finding out what it meant to shut up and do it every day whether she wanted to or not. She said he had taught her that." She gropes for the little plastic cup on the tray of her wheelchair and brings it to her mouth, dribbling bright orange liquid down her chin. "So now you know. Try to tell the real story in your book."

"That's why I'm writing it, Mrs. Aronow. Is this the only one of her journals you've found?"

"I don't want to talk any more. I've talked enough for one day."

He rises, placing the notebook reluctantly on the tray. "I hope you'll let me come again."

"Why not? I don't get that many visitors. But don't you keep after me about those journals. I might take it into my head to burn them, I probably should have done it a long time ago. And he wasn't always like that, either, I don't want to give you that impression. That wouldn't be fair. Like the other time I went to see them, he was fine, they both were. She looked terrific. You'd better put that in, too."

"When was that?"

"I don't remember right now. Come and read to me, that's what I'd like. My eyes are no good any more. And they've got talking books here, but they're all junk. Best-sellers about murders and things. I can't listen to that crap."

"It will be a pleasure. Tell me what you want to hear."

"We used to read to each other at night, my husband and I. All kinds of things. Poetry, of course. And Shakespeare — well, that's poetry too. Start with that. You can wheel me under a tree if it's nice out."

"Shakespeare sounds rather a vague order; have you got something particular in mind?"

"Richard II. King Lear. The Tempest. You choose. And the sonnets. 'For I have sworn thee fair, and thought thee bright/That art as black as hell, as dark as night.' He got it right that time, didn't he? He knew all about it."

10

THE RESTAURANT MONICA HAS CHOSEN FOR BELLE'S party is all deep purples and lavenders, with paisley curtains lined in ivory silk and pale yellow roses floating in pewter bowls. It is a dream of bourgeois elegance, a drip-dry Bonnard that Belle would have scorned in her Marxist days, although later on, when she and Clay were first invited to rich people's houses, she hankered briefly after Persian carpets and glossy chintzes with birds and berries, not for themselves so much as for the sanity they promised. It seemed impossible that lives carried on in such surroundings could be plagued by the disorder, the secret humiliations, that marked her own.

Now she is touched that Monica should have gone to this expense, and touched, too, at the evident pleasure with which she is greeted, the solicitude with which she is led to her place of honor. "We're so glad you're feeling better," a youngish curator says, with what sounds like real fervor, and she understands that they are not, after all, simply waiting for her to die. Maybe the prospect even frightens them a little. Once she is gone, and Ernest, there will be no remnant of the Old Guard. They will be left to flounder on their own, cut off from a past that has lent a certain seriousness to their proceedings.

"A toast," a trustee of the Whitney cries, flushed with alcohol and good will. "A toast to a marvelous show, and may there be many more to follow." It would be niggling to point out that there will be no more shows, at least not of new work, or to ask them why, if they love the paintings so much, they have not bought any for their collections. Her work has been consigned, with due respect, to the status of relic, something on the order of Renaissance bronzes. It is their job, these days, to scout out more daring objects: coffee cups nailed to the wall with twenty-four-carat gold studs, political slogans scrawled on torn bedsheets, photographs of lace nightgowns with blood dripping down their fronts — all the detritus that Marcel Duchamp spawned with that urinal of his. But tonight she is ready to forgive them even that.

Monica, beaming fondly, gives a rambling little speech about how privileged she feels to have mounted this show; Belle bows her head modestly, and then, thank God, conversation breaks out at the separate tables. The waiters bring bowls of cold, greenish soup with dollops of sour cream.

"I'm never quite sure how I feel about melon soup," the man on Belle's right says, a private dealer who sometimes handles Clay's drawings.

She sniffs like the old lady she is. "Fruit isn't something to put in soup." On her left, a fresh-faced young man she vaguely remembers having met in the city is explaining to someone in a high irritable voice how he told Chris he was sorry, he was simply no use in an emotional crisis.

Feeling her gaze on him, he breaks off and turns around. "We have something in common, you know," he says. "I mean, apart from the obvious." Unable to imagine what the obvious might be, she waits impassively for him to continue. "We go to the same doctor, the great Langsbaum."

"You're too young to have arthritis," she says gruffly.

"Of course I'm too young, but try telling that to the arthritis. Anyway, Langsbaum tells me he actually has little children as patients, some of them are crippled with it by age ten. Isn't that horrible?"

She says that it is. She wonders if he too has been injected with gold, and if it proved more effective in his case than her own. Even as they commiserate with each other, the pain is shooting through her hips, the throb in her shoulder makes lifting her spoon more trouble than it's worth. "I've heard that sour cherries sometimes do wonders, you've just got to eat tons of them," he says, and she makes a face.

"I don't need another crackpot cure, thank you." What she needs instead is a more spectacular disease, one that will finish her off efficiently rather than in slow stages. Tomorrow afternoon, the girl with the pink-and-white skin and the incongruous leather jacket will show up at the house to take on her duties, something Belle has hardly let herself think about. When she does, she sees a whole succession of girls, an army of them, trooping through her life from now on, an endless series of houseguests to rob her of her privacy. She will wake to find them at her bedside, spend her evenings listening to their plans for the future. It is this prospect, more than the thought of being lifted from the toilet, that gives rise to feelings of panic.

"Let's talk about something more cheerful," she says when the waiters appear with the rack of lamb, but the subject they hit upon is global catastrophe — the annihilation of the rain forest, the greenhouse effect, nuclear proliferation. It is a distraction of sorts to contemplate the general destruction, grieve for the fate of the planet rather than her own. But the thought of the girl will not be entirely dispelled. Later there will have to be nurses, wheelchair-pushing attendants; she can feel her whole future bearing down in the ache of her joints.

Finally, after white chocolate mousse with a sprig of mint, people push back their chairs and loom over her. Ernest, she notes, is similarly surrounded by admirers, bending low to catch what he is saying. Someone tells her a malicious story about Andrew Danforth and his latest wife, how they accused a houseguest of stealing one of his early drawings, when in fact the maid had taken it down for cleaning and misplaced it. It ought to delight her, as any spiteful report of Andrew always does, but tonight she can barely summon a smile. Her old grudges must be wearing out, like her body.

And the dizziness is back: she tries to ascribe it to the wine she has drunk, but she knows it isn't that. The veins in her head seem to have tightened ominously, as if not enough oxygen is getting through. Maybe her prayers will be answered after all. She beckons to Monica, whose gallery is paying for all this, and tells her she's ready to leave.

"Oh, but you can't." Monica looks distressed. "You can't leave your own party so soon. Aren't you having a good time?"

"I'm having a lovely time," Belle says, patting her hand. "I'm just old and tired, and I need to lie down."

"You'll never be old," Monica says staunchly. But she insists on driving Belle herself, though Belle keeps telling her not to leave her guests. The young man with arthritis helps Belle out of her chair and escorts her slowly to the door. Everyone converges now, to kiss her on the cheek, squeeze her hand till it hurts. She is wonderful, they tell her, over and over, till it feels like a valediction, their last farewell.

"Should I see you upstairs?" Monica asks when they arrive at Belle's door, but Belle tells her to return to the party.

"Are you sure?"

"Of course I'm sure. I'll be fine, I do this all the time." She does not add that after tomorrow that will no longer be true. And so Monica goes, in a flurry of kisses and mutual thank-you's. Now she has only to haul herself upstairs and struggle her way out of her dress, on her own for the last time.

But first she will call her sister, who turned seventy-four today. Naomi, widowed for five years now, lives on the ground floor of a brownstone in Brooklyn, two miles from where they grew up. Her son and her daughter visit her on alternate weekends, so that she can feed her grandchildren ruggelech and exclaim over the paintings they give her, which she affixes to the ice-box with fruit-shaped magnets. When Belle tells her she's had a good life, Naomi hoots at her: "Don't give me this nonsense, *Sheine*. You would have hated such a life, you know that."

"Did I wake you?" Belle asks when Naomi picks up the phone.

"Of course not. You know how it is with my sleeping. I thought for my birthday I would take a pill tonight. That's the best present I could have, a good night's sleep. So how was your party?"

"It was fine. Nice, actually. What do you think about, Naomi, when you're lying there awake?"

"Foolish things. How I didn't invite Mr. Zincke over when his wife died, and I always meant to, and now he's in a home. How I should have tutored Mrs. Heyman's granddaughter in mathematics when she was failing school."

"Your sins."

"Yes, my sins. And you?"

"The same, I guess. So did you hear from all the grandchildren today?"

"Of course."

"And what are they up to? Tell me."

"Joseph has found himself a job for the summer, selling knives door to door. Kitchen knives only. But I wonder if this is such a good idea, in Brooklyn nowadays . . . are you all right, *Sheine*?"

"Of course I'm all right. Except for my joints."

"To take such interest in the news from Brooklyn, it's not like you. I think you must be mellowing. That's what my grandchildren say all the time — 'He's so mellow, it's really mellow.' You know this expression?" And Belle, having rejected *Yiddishkeit* seventy years before, is rescued briefly from loneliness by the inverted sentences of her childhood, with mucousy *ch's* like a catch in the throat.

She says good night to Naomi and begins the climb upstairs, stopping for a minute halfway to look at the painting on the landing, a self-portrait she did two years before she met Clay. The face has a lofty scornful look, the hand is raised, with a paintbrush pointing like a weapon at the viewer. But it is not the face that interests her, of course, nor the stance of the figure; it's the strength of the shapes, that quality that used to make her teachers say she painted like a man. She might have been better off sticking to what she was doing then, instead of battling with modernism, trying so hard to make something new. It had turned, in her case, into a joyless battle. Then she met Clay, and everything changed. Some essential fierceness went out of her work for years. What paintings she produced could only have been done by a woman. And when he died, she could not stop trying to paint his paintings, the ones he would never make. She was not trying to imitate him, as the critics claimed. She was trying to imagine what he would have done next. And she couldn't; nobody could.

She misses his paintings when she is on the Island. In the New York apartment, with its locked steel doors and twenty-four-hour doormen, its wired alarm system that the insurance company demanded, she can keep his paintings all around her, in the bedroom as well as what Ernest calls the salon. Every year she pays a ceremonial visit to the vault to make a new selection. And when it comes to selling them she is stingy, hesitant. She almost says Yes and then beats a skittish retreat. People think it's all a ploy, that she is trying to drive the prices up still further, but it's nothing as devious as that: they are her ghosts, her totems. Nobody will ever earn them as she has, no matter how many millions change hands.

Turning from the portrait, she heads up the stairs, leaning heavily on the railing. She has almost made it to the landing when the dizziness returns, worse than before, and the strength leaves her hand. She feels herself tottering, one foot on the landing and the other on the top step, and then she is falling backwards, her legs crumpling under her, her hands clawing at empty space. Just before she comes to rest on the floor in the hallway, her cheek smashes against the bannister, and pain shoots through her head like sunlight.

For a minute, she still believes she is intact, that the black zig-zags dancing before her eyes will fade any second now. She even thinks she can find her way to the living room, where the phone is, and summon help. But when she tries to lift herself, everything spins around her; her stomach heaves; her eyes will not focus; she sees not her painting on the wall but a smeary canvas with a scene from Montmartre on it, a bad imitation of a bad Utrillo, with a splotchy white church and red blobs for the women's dresses, all of it thickly impastoed, a stew of paint.

It is the painting that hung in her hotel room in Paris, where she'd gone to decide if she'd left him for good. And as she was staring at it, her fourth night there, unable to sleep, he was speeding around a curve at ninety miles an hour, whooping with drunken laughter. As she was taking it down, placing it in the wardrobe, he was sprawled on the gravel with a broken neck, while his mistress crawled from the overturned car, screaming his name.

The veins in her head seem ready to burst, there is a buzzing in her ears, blackness rushes in. She tries one last time to lift her head, to look at her younger self, but no image remains: not her painting, or his painting, or the painting in Paris. Nor does it matter any longer: with the cold floor pressing against her, the bones jutting through her flesh, she has ceased to believe in the redemptive powers of art.

11

OUT OF THE FIRST, GENERAL IMPRESSION OF BABEL—
a sea of voices — random words emerge, and then whole sentences, but still her confusion remains. "You always hated my
mother anyway," a man says bitterly, and a woman snaps back,
"She was the one that hated me." A wooden chair scrapes harshly
across the floor. A high keening voice wails and cracks, pleading for
help. Someone seizes Belle's wrist and starts counting.

Meanwhile she is blind and dizzy, climbing and falling; at the
edge of her brain a wave keeps rising, waiting to engulf her. But
still the words come through.

"It's me, Ma, Enoch, can you hear me? I'm right here."

"They're trying to find her a private room."

"I don't think she'd know if she was in a private room or a
phone booth. Not the shape she's in."

"Yeah, but she's a VIP, they've got to do it. I used to live down
the road from her when I was a kid."

"So?"

"So. I don't know. When she was away I'd sneak around her
house looking in her windows. I remember this big picture she had
on the wall, like a kid's fingerpainting."

Something pricks Belle's arm; heat flows in, and then milky
sleep, rolling towards her brain. But she has no intention of going
under. Vigilance seems called for; one of those voices did not sound

friendly. She heaves her way to the surface with vomit in her throat.

"I'm going to plant those flowers for you, Ma, just as soon as you get home. Right next to the porch, like you wanted."

"Jesus, look at that graph. Where's Shostak?"

"He's catching some sleep."

"You'd better get him."

Blood pounds in her ears, in her eyes, alizarin crimson with flecks of black; it seems she will go under after all. But a minute later Shostak arrives on heavy feet, clearing his throat in irritation. She can tell by his breathing, his footsteps, that he is the one who makes the decisions, he will take charge of her fate.

"Who's her doctor?"

"He's in the city. Bernstein or something. Gagnon talked to him before he went home."

"Only nobody knows what he said, right? It's our little coordination problem again. Christ almighty." A noisy exhalation of breath. "Okay. Ringers lactate to D5 normal saline. Now."

Something massive rolling across the floor, clanking, a shudder passes through her bed.

The woman across the room cries out again: "Help me . . . somebody help me."

"It's all right, Ma, I'm here."

"Hurry it up a little." The wave subsides, the roar in her head shuts off; now there is only arctic cold, the bleak taste of metal in her mouth. "What are you doing to me?" she asks, but the words roll around in her head, never reaching her mouth. "Okay," Shostak says, breathing through his nose, "okay, we're in business." Off he goes, with his weighty tread, before she can tell him they are not in business after all; she is sinking again, drowning, the redness is pulsing and roaring in her head.

"What are you doing here?"

"I couldn't just drive back to the city without knowing what happened."

"You shouldn't be here."

"I wanted to see her, just once. I wasn't going to let her go without ever laying eyes on her."

"You only want to see her because of him, that's all."

"Ssshhh. She might hear us."

"But it's true."

"I don't see what difference it makes."

"Of course it makes a difference. You don't care about her. And you're all wrong. She's wonderful, he was lucky to have her. I wish you'd go."

"I'll stay and keep you company. Hold her hand. Go ahead. She might feel it, you never know. She might hear us, too, that happens sometimes. My father could hear everything even when he was in a coma."

"How do you know?"

"I could tell, that's all. And once when I told the doctor to leave him alone, he squeezed my hand."

"He couldn't really have been in a coma, then."

"Yes, he was. Don't be mad at me."

"It's just that I keep thinking I should have been there. If I'd gotten there one day early she'd be okay."

"She might still be okay."

With a great effort, Belle opens her eyes, but neither of them notices; the man brushes a strand of hair from the girl's face, and she catches hold of his hand to press it clumsily to her cheek, looking at him in a way she cannot mean anyone else to see. She has forgotten about Belle, but Belle herself is remembering something, a piercing sweetness that attaches itself to no object at all. Now the girl's lips are moving, but Belle cannot catch the words; she hears instead another voice, growly and guttural, the fragment of memory rising to the particular, though she cannot place it.

"I had no need of blessing, and Amen stuck in my throat." Where did it come from, that voice? She struggles to remember, but then it dissolves; the heat is back, and the room is filled with a glowing whiteness, the brightness of winter suns. The man's bearded face floats in a sea of light, like Jesus in an old painting, the girl's skin has turned translucent. "Help me," Enoch's mother groans, and the man pulls his hand away and turns to stare; in the ordinary light that is restored, the memory breaks through.

Marcus Sokolow, her first, tyrannical love. He was mournful with intelligence, ancient with it; his voice seemed to throb with all the sorrows of all the Jews who ever lived. After he told her what Plato said about the pre-existence of the soul, she was certain that his own had passed through many lifetimes, though she would not dare say so for fear of incurring his scorn. She should guard against mere temperament, he told her reprovingly, when she showed him her drawings, against cultivating sensibility at the expense of intellect. If she was going to be a true artist, she needed to develop more analytical rigor. He recommended that she study Greek.

And he was always quoting people to her, Fichte and Marx and Schelling, in his guttural melancholy voice that was full of shadows, cadences from that Old Country he had never even seen. All her life she would retain certain things he told her, how Hegel refused to doff his hat to royalty, and Nietzsche's Theory of Eternal Recurrence, as though they were fragments of himself he had handed over, clues to parts of him they both knew were beyond her.

Only very rarely did he talk about himself, with a strange mixture of gloom and conceit. It was his peculiar misfortune, he explained, to be almost a genius but not quite, to have no transcendent gift, only many half-gifts that taken together did not amount to a destiny. He would have to settle for being useful, for pedestrian good deeds, even if it meant a lowering of consciousness. And then, having proved himself worthy, like a medieval knight, he could claim, triumphantly, the love of that ideal female whose image he had been perfecting since he was thirteen years old.

She would be beautiful, of course, but not in any vulgar way, not the sort of woman men stared at on the street, but a high-strung, ethereal being, a person who kept her secrets to herself. And she would have ivory skin, gray-green eyes with long dark lashes; that, somehow, was important. There was never any mention of analytical rigor.

For two whole years, long after she'd given up hope, Belle lived with her vast yearning, supposing him oblivious to her suffering. Once, though, when he had made her cry for no reason, and she told him it didn't matter, he said sternly, "Of course it matters, it could never not matter," adding, "It won't last forever, you know. When you get older you won't love me anymore." But she knew that wasn't true. He was her revelation, the dizzy height of her wanting; not to love him would be to consign herself to darkness.

After leaving Brownsville, he solved the problem of making himself useful by racing through law school in two years and pitting himself against the powers that be. In Kentucky, Alabama, North Dakota, he defended the rights of the miners and the Negroes and the dispossessed farmers. When in New York, he addressed auditoriums full of comrades, exhorting them furiously to join his fight, to leave those airless rooms where they battled among themselves and take up arms in the real struggle. She read about these speeches in *The Daily Worker*; some instinct of self-preservation always stopped her from going to see him in person. Even after all those years, all the men she had brought home to bed, she knew it would not be safe to hear his voice again.

Later she read about his split with the Stalinists over the Moscow Trials, and then nothing until after the war, when he emerged as an alternative to the Ford Foundation. For after a stint with Army Intelligence he had married the romantic female of his imaginings, a tall shy heiress whose poems appeared at long intervals in the literary journals, and had used her money to create a grants program in her family's name. This he administered himself, awarding large sums for projects too esoteric for the others — unlikely physics experiments, art schools in the slums, translations of the Eastern European writers murdered by the Nazis. In one of her more desperate fantasies, Belle even imagined approaching him for money for Clay.

It was the last winter before Clay died. His hands shook uncontrollably; he cried silently, for hours, even when he was sober, which was only in the morning. In a last try at a cure, though she no longer believed in cures, she had managed to borrow an apartment for them in the city, on MacDougal Alley, so that he could see his shrink uptown three days a week. Despite these visits, and Belle's ministrations, and the adulation of the younger painters, the knot in his forehead that had once appeared only when he was talking about something important was present now even in his sleep. All she had managed to accomplish was to make a public spectacle out of his self-destruction.

One night when he was out roaming the bars, and she had cystitis and stayed home, she started fiddling with the knobs on the television in the living room, a novelty item in those days, and there on the screen, as though summoned by magic, was Marcus Sokolow. For a moment she had the eerie feeling that if she turned another dial her father would appear, or the herring women from the Pritkin Street market. He looked as morose as when she had known him, in an elegant dark suit; even his face, an old man's at seventeen, had hardly changed, except that the furrows along his nose had grown deeper. "It's perfectly clear that a revolution in our thinking is called for," he was saying irritably, while his interviewer tried to maintain his fixed smile. "The Greek model, the Renaissance model, the Enlightenment model have been exhausted, however nostalgic we may be for them. What's required is something far more inclusive."

He sounded as stern and abstract as ever, as innocent of the world's ordinary foolishness and pettiness as he had always been. She felt unreasonably glad that he had managed to come through unscathed, that he could still be so sure of anything. And she remembered, as though it were an image of beatitude, lying on her bed, aged sixteen, grappling with the enormous fact that he did not love her.

It seems to her she carried her wanting like a fever all her life;

that was what had defined her, the hunger for some radiance that could never be granted. Other women had children, she had longing. That night on MacDougal Alley she had known that she did not love Clay anymore, he had finally defeated her, but she knew, too, that in some strange way it no longer mattered: the glory rested wholly in her now. Afterwards she played out her part as conscientiously as ever, she fought for his life as though it were her own, but she understood that he was not, after all, her soul. Her soul had pre-existed him; it would survive his death, which could not be put off much longer.

If she is going to die, it might as well be now, with these two beside her to make the blessing. They will do, they are good enough. The roar in her ears grows louder; the light metamorphoses again, turns seashell pink, then bright, a blaze that should hurt her eyes but doesn't. And for the first time in years, joy courses through her; the wave rushes in, lifts her up, fanning out wider and wider.

So this is what she wanted, after all, this is what she has been waiting for all these years.

And then Shostak reappears out of nowhere, with a whole army behind him, their footsteps pounding across the floor, their bodies surging to her side. "Hurry it up," Shostak yells in a hoarse voice, and a huge machine, like a tank, shudders towards her. The room itself gives a vast heave, and something, shockingly, comes crashing down on her chest, so heavy she is afraid her bones will shatter. She gives a scream, or tries to, her back arches, heat floods into her hip, her groin, shoots towards her brain, she cannot breathe from the pain, but a moment later it sinks again, spreads into a fierce ache. The heat recedes, her nerve endings uncurl. "Shit," says a voice above her head, while across the room the woman howls her plea for help. She is back in the unlovely land of the living.

12

ON THE OUTSKIRTS OF AN ANCIENT VILLAGE, HIGH above the vine-dotted slopes of the Loire Valley, stands the Château Ste. Hilaire, a honey-colored castle set in a thousand acres of garden and forest. Swans and ducks paddle in its lily-strewn canals, roses bloom in weathered stone urns on the terrace overlooking the river. In 1569, a saintly princess, in retreat from the corruption of the court, was poisoned in one of its bedrooms by her own mother. Here, protected by moat and turrets, surrounded by Poussins, Ingreses, and the Gobelin tapestries that came with the estate, Rosie Dreyfus, a citizen of France since 1957, a Chevalier de l'Ordre des Arts et des Lettres since 1972, has just entered her ninetieth year.

Three decades ago, her only child, who had never been present at those parties of hers, killed herself at the age of twenty-six; shortly afterwards, though the connection between the two events is not wholly clear, Rosie sold her collection of modern art and retreated into the unreclaimable past. She wanted tranquility, she said, she wanted grace and order and the sanity of the Old Masters, although some people claimed that she had merely lost her nerve.

With the encroachment of age, she has become half-deaf, half-lame, three-quarters blind; she would like to be wise, too, and majestic in the grief for her daughter that threads its way through her dreams. But sometimes, despite her best efforts, the old resentments erupt in her again. A minor bit of slander is enough to open the wound — a snide mention of her sex life or her gallery in a book that someone has sent her, a slighting reference to her taste, a misquotation or an inflated price, and the thirst for vengeance returns. It is then that some supplicant for an interview, whom she may have ignored for months, is likely to get a letter summoning him into her presence.

And so Mark Dudley, singled out in this fashion, finds himself, on a morning in June, being marched by a scornful French secretary through a long tiled gallery, up a carved mahogany staircase, through an ancient set of double doors. Here, in a chamber dominated by a tapestry showing the martyrdom of Saint Sebastian, Rosie awaits him in an agitated state, her silk turban awry on her bony head, her breath coming faster than seems healthy.

She is sitting bolt upright in a brown leather chair with a sloping footrest and a lever at the side to make it recline, an object seemingly transposed from the American suburbs. Her pale skin is fantastically wrinkled, an abstract design of criss-crossing lines; her lips are loose and wet, liver-colored. But her dress is a work of art, a long purple caftan embroidered with flowers and birds and butterflies, with flowing sleeves from which her hands protrude like small withered animals.

"Is he here?" she asks excitedly, and then tells the secretary to leave them; on her way out, the woman tells Mark in a loud voice that he had better speak up, Madame is quite deaf. "Thank you, Marie-France, that will be all," Rosie says, and leans in his general direction, though her eyes do not focus. "Sit down, sit down." He perches on a carved Chinese chair and launches into an expression of gratitude for the interview, but she cuts him off with a wave of her hand.

"Have you read this latest book, by that woman Sondberg?"

"*Method from Madness* . . . yes, of course."

"I want you to know it's all lies."

"I'm sorry, ma'am, I'm not quite sure what you mean."

"It's clear enough, isn't it? I'm saying she's lying."

"About what?"

"About everything . . . everything. Call Marie-France, would you? Use that buzzer over there."

He jumps up and presses the raised button in a large velvet bellpush that is dangling at her side, within easy reach. An instant later Marie-France reappears, looking grim.

"Did Madame require something?"

"I want you to bring that book you were reading to me the other night. There's something in there I want this man to hear. Hurry up now, go get it."

Alone with her again, he makes another try at conversation, murmuring something about the beauty of her château, but once again she shushes him. "Lies," she says, "all lies," breathing heavily, and drums her fingers on the armrest until Marie-France returns.

"Read that part to him. You know the one I mean."

Marie-France clears her throat. "Perhaps Monsieur would rather read it himself."

"Why should he want to do that? You read it."

"On one occasion," Marie-France begins, "Rosie Dreyfus lured the painter Herman Metzger into her palatial bedroom with the promise of a show of his work to be held at her gallery that spring. Later, Metzger told some friends that he 'wouldn't care to repeat the experience.' His comment may have gotten back to Rosie, because she canceled her plans for a show of his paintings with a brutal note telling him that his work lacked grandeur. 'It is my policy to show only geniuses, and you are not a genius,' Metzger remembers her as having written."

"Thank you, Marie-France, that will be all," Rosie says, and the woman bangs the book shut and exits. Again Rosie leans forward, so far that he thinks she may fall.

"All lies," she says, and a spray of spittle comes in his direction. "Every word of it."

"Would you mind if I taped you, ma'am?"

"Of course not. I want it on record. I knew that woman's father, what's his name Sondberg, he wanted me to give him a show, and I wouldn't. He had no gift, a little skill, yes, there was a feel for composition there, a sort of talent I suppose, but it wasn't enough. That's why she's writing about me like that. But they all hate me."

"Why do you think that is?"

"How should I know? We were not nice people, Mr. Dudley. None of us."

"Would you say that was true of the Maddens also?"

"The Maddens. She was a very ambitious ugly woman who couldn't get a man. And he was like a mental patient. Couldn't even talk like a normal human being. Could barely dress himself. She moved in on him, you see, the way women like that do, and maybe it was all for the best. She took control, at least. Somebody had to. But that's not why I got you here. I wanted to tell you about Herman Metzger. He was the one who kept trying to seduce me, and I told him I only slept with geniuses. That's where the line really comes from."

"I'll certainly make a note of that. But if we could just come back to the subject of Clay Madden for a moment . . ."

"She came and sat on my bed."

"Who did?"

"You know. Her. She sat on my bed until she got the money out of me."

"For his allowance, you mean?"

"No, I was already giving him the allowance then. For that ghastly house he wanted. I had pleurisy, I was nearly dying, and she kept barging into my room to hound me about it. I never slept with that man Sondberg either, you know."

"I'm sure you didn't."

"They all pretended I slept with them, they told each other ugly stories to cheer themselves up. Actually, I preferred the homosexual artists. They were much less trouble. And fun, too. They gave wonderful parties. The heterosexuals never gave parties, they expected me to do it."

"If you could just tell me a little more about your association with Clay Madden . . ."

"I don't feel like it. Maybe some other time."

"Of course it's up to you, but you must realize I can't write this book without some account of your dealings with him. I thought you'd rather I got the facts from you."

"I've told it a thousand times. I discovered him, I gave him his first show, you know all that. And then she made me give him an allowance. I couldn't give the paintings away, and I was paying him to do them."

"You were the first to have faith in his work."

"It was her more than anything else. You couldn't get rid of her until you said yes. The same thing with the house. She went and lived with him in that horrible place, way in the middle of no-where. Without electricity. A city rat like her. Pathetic. You had to wonder what it was like for her, whether she almost went mad, too. Not that I cared, I just wondered. She's lucky he didn't kill her out there. I think he tried to."

"When was that?"

"I wrote the check just to get rid of her. And she never even said thank you, just snatched it from me and left. That was what she was like. Her parents sold old clothes, you know, door to door, out in Brooklyn somewhere. She had no schooling at all, she didn't have the shoes to go to school. But she always had a nose for money, I'll grant her that. One of those greedy little *Ostjuden* who give the rest of us a bad name."

"I seem to remember you took her to court after he died."

"Oh my God. That lawsuit. There's a book that came out a few years ago that told the most scandalous lies. Have you got the machine on?"

"Of course."

"Good. I want you to print every word . . . They say I'd given those paintings away, all the ones I was promised under the con-tract, or sold them for peanuts, whatever. When the fact is I simply never took half the paintings I was entitled to, I had no place to put them. There was a very clear understanding that they would keep them for me, and if they could sell them, fine, I'd give them a commission. It never occurred to me to get it in writing. He wasn't a thief, you know — a lunatic, yes, God knows, but not actually a criminal. But *her*. She had some very sharp lawyers."

"So you're saying she lied to the court?"

"*Lied?* It was more than a lie, it was a whole opera she staged for the judge's benefit. Got herself up like the poor widow out of vaudeville, in a dress made from sacking and a hundred-year-old coat. Didn't even wear stockings. My God, Edith Head couldn't have designed it better. And there I was in my Chanel suit and my fur coat . . . it was diabolical. Because of course she was a lot richer than I was by then . . . she's worth millions, you know, she stashes greasy dollar bills under the bed. Anyway, her little scheme worked. I lost. And then she had the nerve to send me a drawing, can you believe that? One measly little sketch he'd done the year he died, when she owed me two dozen paintings."

"What did you do with it?"

"I sold it, of course. It paid for a very nice little Ingres nude, or at least part of one."

"Do you still own any of his paintings?"

"None. Not one. I couldn't look at them any more, I couldn't look at any of those people's work. I'd get up in the middle of the night and turn the lights on and look, and it frightened me. It felt like an assault. His was worst of all. Because of course he really was mad, he wasn't just playing at it, and there's something very frightening about that. Art shouldn't be mad, it has to keep us sane. That's what I started to think, though everyone said I was mad myself. And then one day it wasn't funny anymore. You should see my van Dyck, and the Poussins. I'll have Marie-France show you around before you go. People don't realize what van Dyck could do with a sky."

"There's nothing further you'd like to tell me about Clay Madden?"

"I never knew him," she says. "Never wanted to. He was the kind of person you stay away from as much as possible."

But later that evening, long after Mark Dudley has gone, she has an unsettling memory of Clay Madden, whom she has not thought of, not really, in years. He has become a series of vignettes — of drunkenness, surliness, bad behavior at her parties, maddening silences; a grunting, sweating figure from a bad movie, with no connection to the things he made. Now she remembers a day back in the early fifties, when he had come to town to buy paint and see one of his innumerable shrinks, and he paid a visit to her gallery.

She was there alone, her latest assistant having stormed out the day before; she was on the telephone, complaining to her sister, in desultory fashion, about the depredations of some lover, when he appeared in the doorway in a tweed jacket that seemed to be too tight for him, turning some small object over and over in his hand. She got off the phone and waited for him to speak, but he only looked at her helplessly, his forehead screwed up into a mass of tiny lines. "Did you want to see the show?" she asked, simulating an elaborate patience. He shook his head. He looked out the window for a moment, and then back at her; he was squinting as though the light hurt his eyes. For a minute she was afraid he had come to harm her. "What's that you've got in your hand?" she asked suspiciously, and he opened it mutely, holding out an ordinary smooth gray stone.

Finally, when they had been looking at each other for a good three minutes, she said, "What is it? Did you want to see me for some reason?" and he nodded.

She shut her eyes. "I really can't play this guessing-game, you know. I wish you'd tell me."

"It's about your daughter," he said. It had been ten weeks since her daughter's death. The funeral, the letters of condolence, all the flowers were behind her; the great changes — the move to France, the sale of her collection — would not come for another eight months. She could not imagine what he could possibly have to tell her.

"I met her once. That day I was hanging the mural at your house. She was like me," he said, and stopped.

"I don't know what you mean."

"She had no skin," he said. "It wasn't your fault, she was born that way. I could see. I've been thinking about her." His forehead smoothed out, but there was a jagged line running through his eyes now. "I came to tell you I'm sorry. But maybe she's all right now. Maybe she's better off."

"Would you like a cup of coffee?" she asked, and he gave a little croaking laugh.

"Sure. A cup of coffee, that ought to do it."

She went into the back room, where the hot-plate was, and returned with two mugs of re-heated espresso on a tray. He was making his way around the room, looking at the paintings of the young man her last assistant had discovered. "What do you think of them?" she asked, and he shrugged.

"He might do something good some day. I can't tell."

"And what about your work? Is it going well?"

He shook his head. "I haven't done any real painting for a year."

"I'm sorry," she said, echoing him, and again he shrugged.

"It probably won't make much difference in the scheme of things."

Then someone came into the gallery, a woman she knew slightly, wearing a particularly gorgeous Lilly Dache hat in a fiery shade of red, and he gulped down his coffee and left quickly, with a little wave.

It was the last time she saw him. The following spring she left the country, and the next she heard he had died in spectacularly messy fashion on a country road. That was the summer she moved into the château, the summer she bought her first Poussin and had her daughter's ashes buried in an urn beside the lake. The news of Clay Madden's death had not seemed important at the time, just one more bad ending to be gossiped over with visitors from

America, but now she wishes she had told Mark Dudley about that afternoon in the gallery. After the woman in the red hat left, she went into the bathroom and cried for a long time.

In the light from her Sèvres lamps — she will not have them switched off, even when she sleeps — she can just make out the velvet bellpush that is always draped over her bed when she retires. Stretching out her arm, she fumbles for the button that will summon Marie-France to take a letter.

13

FOR FOUR DAYS NOW, LIZZIE HAS BEEN SLEEPING alone in the house by the cove, waiting for word that Belle Prokoff can come home. When she wakes in the night, in her narrow bed in the guestroom, the silence is so dense she feels as though she has fallen out of time. In daylight, it is the smell of wood she notices most, and the uncluttered spaces. It is a house startlingly empty of machines — no computers, blenders, telephone answering devices; there is not even a television, only a portable radio perched on the deal table in the living room and another in the kitchen. She is ashamed of the Apple she brought from the city, with its nasty plastic smell, its bleeps and red lights, and relegates it to the back of the closet.

"Maybe tomorrow," the doctors tell her every morning, and so she hangs on, scrupulously refraining from rolling back the lid of the ancient desk or rifling through the closets or in any way behaving like the snoop she longs to be. On the landing at the top of the stairs is a portrait of a frowning young woman, executed in large fierce brushstrokes. Her face is mostly swirls of color, with an eye roughly blocked in that somehow adds to her look of scorn; she is wearing a red dress and holding a paintbrush. Lizzie has checked the signature, a faint BP in the lower right-hand corner, and always stops to stare at it on her way upstairs. Sometimes, lingering in the hallway, she imagines opening the drawers of the weathered oak dresser under Belle's bedroom window and finding a whole cache of love letters tied with silk ribbon, or old photographs of Belle and

Clay Madden walking hand in hand. But she will not permit herself to hunt for them.

Anyway, during the day, Nina is there to preserve her from sin. Lizzie is convinced that Nina doesn't have to try to be good, she simply is good. The very planes of her face, her gray eyes, even her shining dark hair, austerely parted and falling smoothly to her shoulders, seem to signify a serenity that radiates from within. Lizzie is half in love with her already, though her efforts at conversation keep petering out. Nina concentrates on household chores with a gravity, a singleness of attention, that could equally be applied to prayer.

Finally, on the fifth day, the doctor says "Tomorrow" instead of "Maybe tomorrow," and Nina begins chopping up soup greens and baking pumpernickel rolls; she sets up the special toilet seat, with the raised platform and the supporting bars, and makes a final adjustment to the hospital bed that has been installed in the dining room, cranking its levers and tucking in the blankets. Lizzie, trying to do her share, goes to the kitchen to clean the red saucepan that held the soup and scratches its enamel with steel wool. Nina assures her that it does not matter, though she looks a little sad.

The next morning, before they leave, Lizzie stands watching Nina plump up the pillows on the red velvet couch and arrange them in a heap at the corner.

"Is that how she likes them?" she asks anxiously.

"Oh, no," Nina says. "I just do it for myself. She doesn't notice one way or another, she's got her mind on higher things. I'm just going to pick some flowers, and after that we can go. That's one thing she does care about, having flowers around, and planning the garden. We have big discussions about border plantings." It is the longest speech Lizzie has heard her make.

"I don't even know what border plantings are."

"But you probably know about the higher things. You can talk to her about them."

* * *

"Well, you've certainly gotten yourself into a mess," Belle says derisively that evening, when she and Lizzie are alone.

"What do you mean?"

"It's not exactly the job you signed on for, is it? Playing nurse to a bedridden old woman."

She is ensconced in the hospital bed downstairs, where Lizzie and Nina installed her before Nina left for the night. It was Nina, however, at Belle's request, who helped her to undress, while Lizzie was shooed out into the kitchen.

"I don't mind," Lizzie says, conscious of the feebleness of this response. "And anyway it's mostly just bruises. You'll be fine in a week or two. They said so."

"Hand me one of those yellow pills. I may be fine in a week or so. Or I may have a blood clot in my brain. That can happen with concussions. And I'm old, I'm not going to heal the way you would. I'm just telling you to think it over. It's going to be extremely boring at best, and it could be a lot worse. I won't blame you if you decide to go."

"But then who'll look after you?"

"Some sort of nurse, I suppose. Don't imagine you're indispensable. You don't even look strong enough to be any good to me. What happens if I have to go to the bathroom in the night?"

"Nina bought a bedpan."

"You weren't hired to empty bedpans," Belle snaps. Lizzie remembers Paul saying the very same thing, and blushes.

"I don't mind," she says again, more staunchly this time. "Really, it's no good thinking about it now, anyway. We might as well see how it works out."

"All right. But you look like the squeamish type to me. I don't want you playing martyr. You can leave any time you want. No hard feelings, no reproaches. And I'll pay you two weeks' wages. What have you been doing with yourself for the past few days?"

"I read a lot," Lizzie says. "I joined the library in town. And I went for walks along the beach."

"Would you like me to get you a television?"

"No, honestly. I'd rather you didn't."

"I have no objections to them myself, it's just that I never acquired the habit of watching. So you really didn't miss the city?"

"Not a bit."

"You must be a different breed from me, then. I hated it here when we first moved out. Especially the quiet. It was like something out of a horror movie, right before the guy comes up the steps with the ax and murders them all. I even missed the noise of the buses outside my window. But you probably didn't grow up in a city."

"No."

"You're not very forthcoming. If we're going to live together we might as well talk to each other. So where did you grow up?"

"In Fairfield," Lizzie says, and Belle laughs.

"What's so funny?"

"I knew it was Connecticut. Were you rich?"

"Not really rich, just sort of comfortable, you know? I mean, where money wasn't a worry."

"And what was a worry?"

Lizzie hesitates; only the sneer about Connecticut makes her say what comes next.

"My mother was knocked down by a car when I was fourteen, and she never really recovered. They kept operating on her, and trying different medicines, but so many different parts of her brain had been damaged the doctors never knew what would go wrong next. Sometimes she'd see double, or she'd lose her balance suddenly, or her speech would be fine one minute and slurred the next. And then she started bleeding into her brain, and she died." It is the first time she has told this story so flatly, with dry eyes, or failed in the telling to say how gallant her mother was, how she made a joke of things until almost the end. She feels ashamed, as though she's been showing off, trying to prove to Belle that she too knows something about suffering.

"I'm sorry," Belle says.

"It's all right."

"Of course it's not all right . . . What about that man who was with you in my hospital room?"

"Oh, God, you saw him."

"Why shouldn't I have seen him? He was right by my bed. So who is he?"

"A painter."

"Ah. I remember now. You accused him of only wanting to see me because of Madden. Not the first time that's happened, but thank you."

"You're welcome."

"He had an accent, didn't he?"

"He's Australian."

"I don't think I've ever met an Australian painter. So did you take him to the studio while he was here?"

"Yes. He drove me out that afternoon, you see, to start work, and the house was empty, and then we went next door and your neighbor said you'd been taken to the hospital. So I got him to drop me off there, but then he came upstairs. I didn't mean him to."

"Did you take him to the studio before or after you came to the hospital?"

"After . . . why?"

"I'm trying to reconstruct events. I'm interested in your character, since it seems I'll need to rely on you. Tell me about your course at Columbia. You can't just be studying the art of the nineteen forties."

"I'm mostly doing English literature, actually. With a specialty in the nineteenth century."

Belle gives her a sharp look. "I thought you came here to interview me about a thesis on art history."

"I know . . . that was Heather, really. I just sort of came along to keep her company."

"So you deceived me."

Lizzie bows her head; she wonders if she should explain about Paul and Clay Madden, but lacks the nerve.

"Never mind. How do you get along with Nina?"

"I think she's wonderful."

"Good. Well, if you're going to stay here for a while, you might as well invite your Australian for a weekend. That should keep you from getting bored."

"That's very kind of you," Lizzie says primly, and then the phone rings; she jumps up and hurries through the open doors into the living room.

"Take a message. Say I'm fine and take a message."

"Prokoff residence," she says, as she has been saying all day. Since Belle got back, the phone has rung a dozen times — someone from the Guggenheim, from the Walker Art Center, the Rose Museum at Brandeis, several galleries in New York; none of the callers, Lizzie notes, identifies herself through name alone, but always by affiliation. Belle has directed her to take down their numbers and say she will get back to them when she is well enough.

"May I then speak to Miss Prokoff?" a man says irritably.

"I'm sorry, she can't come to the phone right now."

"Why not?"

"Because she can't get out of bed."

"Is that Nina?"

"No, it's Lizzie."

"And who are you?"

"I'm the graduate student Miss Prokoff hired to help out for the summer."

"Right . . . then kindly tell me how she is."

"Who the hell is it?" Belle calls out.

"May I tell Miss Prokoff who's speaking?"

"You may. It's Ernest. Ask her when she's going to get a phone by her bed, for God's sake."

"It's Ernest. He wants to know when you're going to get a phone by your bed."

"Tell him I'll think about it. Say I'll phone him as soon as I can."

She relays this message to Ernest, but he persists. "What precisely is her condition?"

"She's just bruised her spine, that's all, and her hip. And had a concussion. Nothing is broken except a rib."

"I know that, young lady. I've been phoning the hospital twice a day. I mean what is her precise condition as of this moment?"

"She's in bed," Lizzie says desperately.

"You told me that already. Is she fully conscious? Is she in pain? Can she move?"

"She can move, but it's very hard for her."

"Thank you, that was most informative," Ernest says, and hangs up.

"My God," Lizzie says, returning to Belle's side. "What a mean man."

"He's one of my dearest friends," Belle says. "He's kept me sane for years. Give me another yellow pill; this one isn't working."

"You only took it a few minutes ago."

"None of them work," Belle says, grimacing. "What day is it today?"

"The eleventh."

"You're sure?"

"Yes."

"Then it's my wedding anniversary. My forty-first. Imagine that." She looks mockingly at Lizzie, raising an eyebrow.

"Did you get married out here?" Lizzie asks timidly, that being the most neutral question she can think of.

"No, we got married in one of those poky little towns on the Hudson. A place called Ardsley."

"Was that where your parents lived?"

Belle laughs. "No, it was where I found someone who would marry us. He wanted to get married in a church, but I was a Jew and he hadn't been to church in fifteen years, so they all said no. Then a Unitarian minister in Ardsley said he'd do it, so we took the train up there."

"Just the two of you?"

Belle looks at her suspiciously. "Why are you asking these questions?"

"I'm trying to imagine what it was like."

"You can't. It was such a different time. There was a war on. And even people were different then." Her voice is suddenly groggy, as though the pill might be kicking in after all. A minute later her head droops onto her chest; Lizzie is about to tiptoe out when Belle speaks again, her words slurring together.

"The minister looked like Ichabod Crane . . . I kept looking at his nose, thinking, This can't count, this isn't a real marriage. But he was a good man, very good . . . you can't . . . and then a dog followed us to the station, a little collie, he was afraid it wouldn't find its way back. The woman was tending the graves behind the church, she came in to be our witness, she brushed the dirt off her hands. Afterwards he told us always . . . always to forgive each other . . . do you see. Do you, Belle . . . I felt like I was confessing to a crime. Do you, Belle, take this man . . ."

Her voice trails off. Lizzie imagines her standing very straight, shoulders flung back, jaw thrust forward: Do you, Belle . . . do you, Belle, take this man to be your lawful wedded husband? Yes I do.

14

SHE HAS TRUE CAT'S EYES, BLUE-GREEN AND GLINTING, in a face that seems to be collapsing as he watches; the skin on her jaw wobbles perilously each time she smiles. But the smile itself, sweet and fluttery, is unchanged after thirty years. She was wearing the same smile, along with flowered shorts and a halter top, in the snapshot that is her single claim on posterity.

It is the last photograph of Clay Madden, taken the week before he died. He is no longer the lean cowboy with the cigarette drooping from his mouth, but a puffy-eyed dazed-looking man with a bad haircut, his forehead screwed up in pain. Slumped behind the steering wheel of his car, he stares out the window, while Marnie Ryan, seated on the hood, waves flirtatiously at the camera. It is obvious, in retrospect, that he was about to die — it was obvious, according to many witnesses, at the time — but not at all clear what she thinks she is doing there, with her long painted nails and her sex-kitten pose, unaware, seemingly, that the man beside her is in a state of terminal despair.

"I don't have anything to offer you, I'm afraid," she says, a little crossly, but when he suggests that they might go out somewhere for a drink, she brightens immediately.

"Oh, that would be lovely. But I can't go out like this . . . do you think?"

"I don't see why not," he says gallantly, though of course he does see: her long batik skirt is covered in cat hairs, like the seat she has ushered him to, a sagging armchair half-covered by a dingy red shawl.

"Well . . . it would be fun, wouldn't it? Wait here for one sec, and I'll change." He occupies himself in prowling the room, confirming its resemblance to numerous places he used to smoke dope in during his brief time at the Leicester Polytechnic. Though Marnie Ryan is recognizably a product of the fifties, inveterately girlish in the manner of that decade, her furnishings — a faded Indian bedspread on the couch, velvet wall hangings with spangles in many colors, a white Afghani rug embroidered in blue and pink — evoke the less ordered decade that followed. Everything looks limp, exhausted, as though it has had to do more service than it was created for. He knows from his researcher that a year after Madden's death she married a nineteen-year-old N.Y.U. student but left him after a few months; in 1969 she moved in with her yoga teacher and later opened a bed-and-breakfast with him in the Virgin Islands. For the past twelve years she has subsisted on a meager legacy from a brother she nursed through cancer and her earnings as a part-time proofreader for a medical journal.

Finally, when she does not emerge after ten minutes, he approaches the peeling white bookcase in the corner and selects from among the volumes of Kerouac and Kenneth Patchen and Ginsburg what seems to be her most up-to-date purchase, the first volume of Carlos Castenada. Turning to the opening section, he starts reading.

She knows that the purple dress she is wearing has a rip under the arm and a stain over the left breast; she knows that her perfume is a little too strong, and that since they arrived at the restaurant, she's been giggling too much, gesturing too dramatically. Even the drink she's just ordered — a Manhattan — is out of date. None of these items of knowledge, however, can help her right now. Long ago she decided that a major difference between men and women was that men never knew when they were making fools of themselves, while women always did. But it seems to be just one more way in which men are better off.

The waitress brings their drinks. She pauses for a moment, to take a sip.

"Would you mind if I recorded you?"

"Here?"

"It's a very small machine, quite inconspicuous. I'll just tuck it away" — he places it deftly behind the chipped bud vase holding a single rose — "and no one will have to know."

"I suppose that would be okay."

"So tell me about Clay Madden."

"Oh no, that's not how you do it . . . you have to ask me questions."

"Why?"

"I'd just feel more comfortable, that's all." She is afraid, now that her drink has come, that she might start babbling. She might veer from the subject of Clay Madden, whom she can't remember very well today, and begin talking about Stuart Hollis, her latest lover, whose phone was answered that morning by a woman with a German accent. She doesn't even like him very much — he tells endless stories about triumphing over his enemies in the office and is finicky about anything pertaining to sex — but she thought at least he'd be too scared of disease to stray. And so she disregarded certain troubling signs — telephones unanswered at midnight, the sudden appearance of a jar of honey and jojoba conditioner in his shower stall, though he is practically bald. It seems like the final humiliation that even he should be cheating on her.

"God bless you," Mark Dudley says, when she sneezes.

"Thank you."

"So tell me about the first time you met him."

And suddenly she remembers, more sharply than she has in years, the particular mood of that day, or herself on that day: a sort of restless, mutinous feeling, after three hours spent trailing behind her friend Carol through one gallery after another. Her feet hurt in their high-heeled sandals, and every time she admired a painting, Carol would point out the flaws in its composition, or say it had been done before, or just make a disapproving face. It was the same with books. Marnie only had to say she'd just read the most wonderful book for Carol to tell her it was actually a watered-down version of some much better book Marnie had never heard of.

One painting Marnie had stopped in front of Carol said was a fake Clay Madden, so Marnie asked who Clay Madden was. "He's just about the greatest painter alive," Carol said solemnly. "The greatest American painter, anyway."

"Have you ever met him?" Marnie asked.

"I've seen him around. He hangs out at the Bristol, same as everyone else."

"Why don't we go there?"

They were drinking ginger ale at a table near the kitchen when Carol nudged her, pointing to a burly man with an unshaven face. "That's him. That's Clay Madden."

"I'm going to talk to him," she said, and stood up before Carol could stop her. It was like being in high school again, doing something on a dare, because nobody else would. Carol might lay down the law about the difference between talent and genius, she might go on about necessary and unnecessary gestures, but she would never have the nerve to actually walk up to Clay Madden.

"I just knew as soon as I saw his paintings," she says now, taking another sip of her Manhattan, "that I had to meet him. It was like they had been painted for me, like they were meant for me to find. And then one night I was in a bar with a friend of mine, she was an actress like me, but she was studying painting, too; she was very knowledgeable about all the arts. And she pointed him out to me, and I just had to go talk to him. I had to let him know how much his work meant to me."

In fact, she had only said "Hello there" — trying it out, seeing if she was pretty enough to pick up this famous man. And then she had been startled by the misery in his face. It made her ashamed of bothering him, when it was clear that he had enough problems already. She turned to leave, mumbling an apology, but he reached out a hand and turned her around again, saying, "Wait, don't go. What's your name?"

Mark Dudley is leaning across the table, looking intently into her face. "I can't seem to get a handle on him, you see. I've got all these facts that I can't put together, like a jigsaw puzzle where all the pieces are there, but they don't add up to anything yet."

"He was a terribly complex man," she says solemnly, because it seems expected of her.

"I know that. But I thought maybe you could help me. I think you might be the key. Tell me what he was really like."

She looks at him uncertainly, puzzled by the extreme sincerity in his voice. "Nobody can ever say what someone else is really like," she says awkwardly.

"Then tell me anything you can. What he said to you that first night, what he told you about his paintings, how he looked at you in bed, anything. Please." He puts his hand over hers, and then it hits her: it's a seduction scene he's playing, that's what the earnestness is for. He is planning to track the scent of Clay Madden across her body — not the first time somebody's tried it, but no one has made this much effort in years. And at least, if he stays with her tonight, she won't be tempted to phone Stuart Hollis at two in the morning.

She cocks her head and smiles at him, a slow, lopsided smile. "I'll tell you something he said to me one night at my apartment. He said that when he was painting, he always heard the wind howling in his head."

"That's really amazing."

"He was an amazing man." In fact, what she has just told him is a lie, like most of her stories about Clay Madden. The truth is that mostly, when he was with her, all he did was cry, though sometimes he wanted to sit and stare at her too. He would ask her to sit in the window seat of her bedroom with the curtains drawn behind her — dark blue velvet curtains, with a tassel fringe, that she had bought at a flea market — and prop himself up on the bed, just watching her. What she could never explain was how he'd made her feel it was a privilege simply to look at her, to run his hands over her skin. It didn't matter what he did or couldn't do in bed: nobody had ever made her feel that beautiful.

"What I meant was, it's an amazingly bleak image, isn't it? A terribly lonely thing to say."

She blinks at him in irritation. "Nobody ever claimed he was Mr. Happy." The spell is broken once again. She is wondering, miserably, if Stuart is with his German right now, and what she looks like, if she is young and tidy and efficient, never has a safety pin in her bra or dirty sheets on her bed.

He notes in drunken detachment the musty softness of her flesh, the creases and folds in her neck. When he kisses her, she breaks away, protesting, but he shushes her with a moan and backs her towards the bedroom. The unmade bed, with its dingy flowered sheets, can be reached only by picking a path through piles of rumpled magazines and a week's worth of underwear. He is reminded again of his student days, when everyone's bedroom looked approximately like this.

At the same time he is thinking, This is the closest I'm ever going to get to Clay Madden, an idea that excites him inordinately, so that he becomes a little rough, tearing at her dress in his impatience. She steps back from him, and tries to lift it over her head, but it snags on the clip of her bra and he has to disentangle it for her. From inside the dress, she makes muffled noises of alarm, while he notes with dismay the rents in her black silk underpants.

But once they are safely in bed, once she is free of all encumbrances and he is burrowing into her rolls of flesh, the thought of

Clay Madden returns. I am stalking his ghost, he tells himself drunkenly, and then an image of Belle imposes itself. There is nothing, he knows, that she would hate more than what he is doing now; there is no better revenge he can possibly take. With this thought, his arousal is complete.

Afterwards, Marnie Ryan collapses on top of him, burying her face in his neck.

"Do you still think about him a lot?" he asks, in a voice carefully full of compassion.

She lifts her head an inch. "Not really. Sometimes. It's been a long time since he died."

"So you don't have nightmares about the accident or anything."

"Not any more. I used to."

"Have you ever really talked to anyone about it? Maybe if you told the whole story, it would help you to understand."

"Oh God," she says peevishly. "There's nothing to understand. It was dark out, and he was drunk, he was laughing like a maniac, and he went off the road. He didn't say anything, he didn't have any great last words for the world. A million people have asked me already. There's nothing left to tell. No secrets."

"But there've got to be. That car crash is legend."

She flops onto her back. "Only because he died, that's why. Everyone wants to make such a romance of it, they have to pretend it was different somehow from all the other car crashes on all the other country roads. Or that it was some kind of symbol for his life. And it wasn't. The only thing that was different about it was the person driving the car. Okay?"

He is impressed by her sudden eloquence, but not convinced. "Of course it was symbolic. It was a violent end to a violent life. The ultimate American death, a hot rod speeding down a dirt road."

"It wasn't a hot rod. Or a dirt road, either. It was tarmac."

"The idea's still the same."

"Then write what you just said to me, that's good enough. You don't need all the gory details."

"But will you tell me in your own words? Exactly what happened?"

"I don't want to think about it right now."

"Not now, then, but another time?"

"Is there going to be another time? Or are you just going to disappear, and I'll never hear from you again?"

"You'll hear from me," he says fervently as she turns back to face him.

"When?" She moves on top of him again, nuzzling his neck.

"Soon," he says, as she wriggles downward on his body. He shifts underneath her, groaning faintly. Next time, he means to find out exactly what happened in that car.

15

One morning a week after Belle's return, Lizzie walks into the kitchen to find Nina at the stove with tears running down her face.

"Don't," Nina says, as Lizzie, fighting off panic, pats her awkwardly on the shoulder. It has never occurred to her that Nina is anything but serenely happy. "Please don't. Please just go away." Her eyes are red and swollen, even her beautiful shiny hair is disheveled. Lizzie goes back to the dining room in a state of acute distress.

"What's happened to my cup of tea?" Belle wants to know.

"I forgot."

"What do you mean, you forgot? That's why you went to the kitchen."

Lizzie hangs her head.

"Stop looking like that," Belle says. "It's Nina, isn't it? What's wrong with her?"

"Nothing."

"Then where is she? Why hasn't she come to say hello?"

Lizzie is silent.

"Tell her to come here," Belle says, "go ahead. And then you take a walk. Go down to the beach. The sea air will do you good."

Lizzie returns to the kitchen to fetch Nina, who looks at her reproachfully. "I didn't tell her anything," Lizzie says, close to tears herself. "She just knew."

"It's not your fault," Nina says sadly, blowing her nose. "It's me. I shouldn't have come in today, I knew that."

"So he's done it again," Belle says, as soon as the front door shuts behind Lizzie.

"He hasn't done anything."

"He's been hitting you."

"That's not true. Look." She turns her face from side to side and then holds up her bare arms, twisting them this way and that. "See? He hasn't touched me."

"Not this time, maybe. But he's done it before, and he'll do it again. Don't tell me different."

"You talk like he's some kind of monster, like he's not even a human being or something. Why do you hate him so much?" The tears are still running down her face. Belle tries a different tack.

"I don't hate him," she says, more gently. "I just want him to behave better. I want him to make you happy. And he doesn't seem to. That's what concerns me."

"Only because he's so unhappy himself," Nina says and bursts out sobbing. "Oh God." She gropes on Belle's night-table for a tissue and wipes her face. "I'm sorry. I hate this, I hate you seeing me like this."

"Don't worry about me," Belle says. "I've seen a few people cry in my time."

Nina lets out a shuddery sigh.

"And I know a thing or two about being a good soldier, too," Belle tells her.

"Yes . . . I know. I mean, people have told me."

"I'm sure they have," Belle says drily. "I'm sure they've told you all sorts of things."

"But I didn't necessarily believe them," Nina says with sudden fierceness. "I knew it wasn't as simple as they made out, I knew you must have had your reasons."

"Everybody has reasons. They're just not very good ones sometimes. That's what I want you to think about."

"What are you saying? That I ought to leave him? As if I

bought a dress and now I'm going to take it back to the store and maybe get something else? I know people who act that way about marriage. I never want to be that kind of person."

"You never will be, believe me." But Nina does not seem to have heard her.

"I think about what I said when we got married — for richer or for poorer, in sickness and in health. Till death do us part. They're not just words, you really have to mean them. And I did. I still do."

Belle is silent for a moment. "Then tell me why he's so unhappy."

"Because no one will give him a chance. There are so many things he's good at, it's just not fair. He can fix things nobody else can, he has all these ideas for building things, he can carve like they did a hundred years ago. He's got this old book with all the different moldings in it, you should see the things he makes just for practice. And . . . I don't know, he just knows about so many things. He can track an animal through the woods like an Indian."

"Unfortunately," Belle says, "that's not a skill that's much in demand these days."

Nina gives her a wounded look. "I don't want to talk about it anymore. What would you like for breakfast? I could make you some pancakes."

"I'm not in the mood for pancakes. Corn flakes will do."

A minute later Nina returns with a tray on which there are not only tea and corn flakes but three pink roses, in a dark blue vase whose two halves Clay had found in the rubble when they first moved out there and glued together, as a peace offering, one morning after he'd come in drunk the night before.

"Do you want me to phone Dick Goodrich?" she asks politely. "He hasn't done any work on the garden since your accident."

"Your husband's a carpenter, right?"

Nina nods warily.

"Then could he do some work for me? I need some railings installed so I can get around. And one of those elevator contraptions for the stairs. I want to move back into my own bedroom."

"Why are you doing this?"

"You said no one gave him a chance. I'm giving him a chance."

"All right," Nina says, after a pause. "I'll ask him."

"Ask him now."

Lizzie, meanwhile, has been scouting out the dunes, doggedly searching for places where she and Paul can shelter undisturbed; she does not like the idea of making love in Belle's house, with Belle, possibly awake, lying in the room below. When she returns to the house, she finds Belle in a particularly cheerful mood, more energetic than she has been since she got home. Lizzie is kept occupied, for the rest of the morning, making lists of people who have phoned, people who have sent cards, people who have sent flowers, and sorting out the bills that have arrived over the past few weeks.

Afterwards, they all sit at the kitchen table, eating Nina's pea soup. "Nina's husband is coming this afternoon," Belle tells Lizzie, and explains about the work she needs done. "And then you and I should adopt some kind of regimen. I want you to buy books for me. What do you recommend? Jane Austen? Do you think I'd like her?"

"Not particularly."

"Well, what should I read? Proust? Henry James? I haven't read them either."

"You could try," Lizzie says doubtfully. It strikes her that Belle is not cut out, somehow, for literature. It is not forthright enough for her, it insinuates too much and declares too little. All those stratagems of indirection by which novels seek to arrive at truth: how can Belle possibly be expected to tolerate such subterfuge? She would be exasperated by Proust, she could never summon the patience for Henry James.

"What about Dreiser?" Lizzie asks, though she doesn't much care for Dreiser herself.

"Why him?"

"I just think you'd like him somehow. Or maybe Dickens."

"Let's start with Dickens," Belle says. "I've read *A Tale of Two Cities*, of course, and the one with Scrooge. We had those in school. Get me something else."

Then she decides to teach Lizzie gin rummy. She is trouncing her at the game for the third time when Nina walks in, followed by a man with blond hair down to his shoulders and bright blue eyes in a gaunt face. "You remember Sam," Nina says shyly, and Belle turns around, cards in hand, to fix him with a beady eye.

"Of course I remember him. Lizzie, this is Sam Hazen. Lizzie Dowson."

"Hello there, Lizzie," he says, blinking rapidly. "Hello, Mrs. Madden. You're looking very chipper today."

"Thank you," Belle says. "How are you these days?"

"How am I, how am I . . . I try not to think about that too much. It's like, how are you, Sam, and then I spend all day wondering how I really am, and where does that get you? My heart's beating, my pulse is regular, what else can I say?" His foot jerks up and down to some internal rhythm. "What's the story with these railings? You want nice ones, polished ones, you want fancy brackets, or will the kind from the hardware store do? And if you don't know what the kind from the hardware store looks like, I've got one here." He holds out a thick curved bracket in raw pine. "You get this kind, you might as well get the poles to match. Just unfinished wooden rods. Or are you looking for elegance?" Meanwhile his eyes wander around the room, settling on nothing in particular.

"Probably not," Belle says. "I haven't really thought about it."

"Hey, you're the artist. I don't want to make you something ugly and then you realize you can't live with it. You want the fancy oak ones, or cherry, they run about double the price. Eight dollars a foot instead of four. You tell me. My labor costs the same either way."

"Let's try oak."

"Oak it is. I can buy it tomorrow and get them up in no time."

"I need a way to get upstairs, too."

"Sure sure sure. Nina told me. One of those little chair elevators, right? Only those you can't buy in oak. I've been looking at catalogues down at the pharmacy. They're all metal, they're ugly as shit, excuse the expression, and they're real expensive for what you get. You'd do a lot better letting me make you one in wood. The old-fashioned kind, like a regular chair, only on gliders. I could make the chair to fit the staircase and just buy a little diddly-squat motor, like for a washing machine, to make it go."

"Are you sure it'll work?"

"Sure I'm sure. You attach the motor to the chair, you run some track going up the stairs, and you're all set. Easy as anything. We just need some lightweight wood for the chair, ash or something, and I get to work."

"How long will it take you?"

"Couple of days. Maybe three. I tell you what, I'll show you the catalogues, and we'll take the cheapest price there is. That's what I'll charge. And if you want I'll even carve the chair for you. Make you a throne."

"You don't have to do that. Just charge me for your time."

"I'd rather do it my way, see if I can come out ahead. It'll make it more interesting for me."

There is a silence, during which Sam's eyes continue to travel around the room. He drums with his fingers on the table. Belle clears her throat. Then he speaks again. "Did you know there was a guy in town asking questions about Mr. Madden?"

Carefully, Belle lays down her cards. "What kind of questions?"

"I don't know. I didn't talk to him. But I ran into some guys at Phelan's he'd been buying drinks for. Plus the pharmacist mentioned it this morning."

"An Englishman?"

"That's right. You know him, do you?"

"I wouldn't say that. I've met him. What did they tell him?"

"I don't know. The same old stuff, probably. You know the kinds of stories they tell about Mr. Madden. And the guy was buying them drinks." He makes a disgusted sound. "Seems he's got some old journals this friend of yours gave him."

"What do you mean? What kind of journals?" All the habitual mockery is gone from Belle's voice. Lizzie stares at her in alarm.

"Some diaries you kept a long time ago. Or that's what he told Lou Prescott." Sam, too, seems very interested in the change in Belle, though not at all discomfited. He is watching her closely, wholly at rest for the first time since he came in.

"Where is he?" Belle says, in the same shrill voice.

"Back in the city, I guess. But he'll be out again. Or that's what he told them."

"Will you bring him here?"

"When he comes back?"

"Yes."

"If he's willing to come. I can't exactly drag him here at gunpoint."

"He'll be willing," Belle says. "Don't worry about that. Just tell him I want to talk to him. He'll come."

16

AT MILO'S, THE AIR CONDITIONER IS ON THE BLINK, which inspires the artists to new heights of wrath: over global warming, the erosion of the ozone layer, the shoddy manufacturing practices in America today.

"Nobody takes pride in their goddamn work anymore."

"How can they take pride in their work when all they're doing is feeding a machine?"

"At least the machine they're feeding is more honest than the one we're feeding."

Paul, sweating copiously, is at the bar, talking to Colin, the painter abandoned by his girlfriend two weeks before. For the past several minutes, they have been squabbling about Belle Prokoff: whether she is suffering from Alzheimer's and will soon be totally out of it, as certain gossips claim; whether she was always a deep-dyed bitch or was driven mad by the art world. Out of his general sourness more than any real conviction, Colin is insisting on her inherent bitchiness; Paul, from loyalty to Lizzie, is defending her. It is a matter of some interest in the bar that he is heading for Belle Prokoff's house the following weekend.

"Never mind, just give my regards to Madden's ghost," Colin says finally, before crossing the room to loom above a crop-haired woman reading Barthes in the corner.

"What do you want?" she asks, looking up from her book.

"I want to talk to you about semiotics."

The next time Paul goes into Milo's, a smirking Colin beckons him over.

"You owe me one, babe. You might even owe me big."

"What are you talking about?"

"Buy me a Guinness and I'll tell you."

Paul buys one for each of them, and carries them, sloshing foam, to Colin's table. "Now tell me."

"You know Sasha Borodin? Used to be with Gershner?" Paul shakes his head. "Well, never mind. The point is, she's starting her own gallery, right there in the Fuller Building. And she's going to put me in a group show next fall. So I went to see her this afternoon, and she was talking about Belle Prokoff, how she's only got three months to live and all that shit." He takes a gulp of his beer. "Man, that is good stuff."

"Go on."

"Well, I told her this friend of mine was headed for chez Madden over the weekend, and she got very interested suddenly. Wants you to phone her."

"That's it? That's why I had to buy you a Guinness for four bucks?"

"Come on. It's a great connection to have. She knows everyone, she's opening a gallery on Fifty-seventh Street, what more do you want? Plus she's the kind who'll make it big, I can tell. A mega Gorgon."

"But she didn't say she wanted to see my work, did she? She's probably just after Prokoff's phone number."

"She knew about your work. She even remembered that critic for *Artnews* who said you'd done an unthinkably subversive thing, or however the hell he put it, and you'd made us slow down and pay attention. You'd be stupid not to phone her."

"Michael Sorenson," Paul says, and then, when Colin looks blank, "The guy from *Artnews*. Never mind. Give me her number." Colin scrawls it on a napkin and pushes it across the table. Paul peers at it suspiciously. "What did you say her name was?"

"Sasha Borodin. It's her only other good point, she's got a sexy name. But don't start fantasizing about exotic Russian Jewesses or shit like that. I tell you, she's a real bloodsucker. Strindberg couldn't have dreamed her up."

Paul is sufficiently impressed to phone Sasha Borodin the very next morning, with the result that, a few days later, he finds himself waved to a striped deckchair in her yet-to-be-opened gallery, all but empty except for a vast, gleaming black desk. Behind the desk, in a black leather chair, is Sasha Borodin herself, looking, with her dead-white skin and dyed red hair, like the vampire of Colin's description. When Paul is seated, she swivels around, turning her back on him. "Listen," she says into the phone, "I don't have time for this shit. Just don't worry about it. Nobody's going to care what you're wearing except some other dowdy little woman with an over-active imagination." Then she hangs up and swivels to face him.

"Right, okay, I know who you are, I just don't remember your first name. So tell me . . . right. Okay, listen up, Paul. I want you to do something for me, and then I might help you out. I saw your show at the Braxton Gallery a few years back, in fact I made a note in my book at the time, I really thought you were going to be hot that season. Bad call, right? But you know how to push the paint around. The one that was playing with the shapes from Cézanne, I still remember that. So I could put you in a group show if you help me out, no problem, and see what happens if we start pushing you a little. Then maybe a two-man show next spring. Are you interested? Of course you're interested. You're hungry, right? You want to be a star. Shit. So you'll do it."

He stares at her helplessly, at her sharp little nose, the circles of bright rouge on her cheeks. Her tongue keeps darting out of her mouth, racing over her lips like a terrier in pursuit of prey.

"You should see your face," she says. "You think I shouldn't talk like that, right? Don't worry, sweetie, I can still bullshit the rich folks when I have to. I'm as good a suck-up as the rest. Only I don't bother with the artists, that'd be a waste of breath. It's like, the art world is the last stronghold of pure capitalism, do you realize that? None of that vertical partnership shit they teach at the B school. There's a hundred thousand suppliers out there, all panting for someone like me to come along and stir up demand. So what you have to do for me is, you have to find out what Prokoff's got. And how you're going to do that I don't know. Check under the beds, eavesdrop on her phone calls, whatever. Be creative. I just got a card from someone that said, 'Have a creative summer,' how's that for disgusting? Are you mute or something?"

"I don't know what you expect me to say. I'm not even sure what you want me to look for. Maddens?"

"Of course Maddens. What else would I be talking about? They won't be hanging in the front parlor, she's not that crazy. But they're somewhere, and no one knows what she's got, not really. There are some stashed in a bank vault, maybe a dozen, everyone knows about those, but I've got a hunch, I think she might be hiding more somewhere. There are still too many unaccounted for, all those early ones that no one wanted. They can't all have been destroyed, or painted over. This guy I knew who used to be her studio assistant, he figured she had a little stash someplace. He could just smell it, you know?"

"What are you planning to do when you find out?"

"Hey, you mean do I want you to roll one up and bring it back to me? That's too much to ask for, right? So just give me the report, and I'll take it from there. I might try to get to her, try to do a show of his early work. There hasn't ever been a decent show of the figurative stuff. But that's strategy, that's not your job. You just bring me the data, and I'll work out the tactics. Where did you get that accent?"

"Where did you get that face?" is what he wants to say. He has got to get out of there soon, before he loses it completely.

"Australia," he says, standing up.

"Oh. It's not very attractive, is it? Sort of a cross between a whine and a snarl. That might be the problem." She looks him up and down speculatively, as though trying to work out whether her collectors might fancy him. "So are you legal here or what?"

"Completely legal."

"Okay. You can sit down again if you want." He perches on the edge of the chair, while she continues talking.

"You haven't gone totally unnoticed, you know, it's just that no one's ever decided to do anything about you. No one's ever positioned you in the marketplace. Braxton was useless, he was too rich to work. It might be interesting to see what would happen if I threw my weight behind you."

"And if I can't find out anything?"

"Then hey, it's been swell meeting you, right? But if you want it bad enough you'll come up with the goods. That's how it goes, it's the American way. So give me a call when you've got news." She picks up the receiver and punches a button. "Listen, sweetie" — she waves Paul out — "I got your text for the catalogue, and you've got to be joking. It's like some creep who picked his nose in geometry class, the poems he published in the school paper."

Then he is back on 57th Street again, where everyone around him seems to ooze money; they all look thin and sleek as whippets, as shiny as gleaming new cars. It is a windy afternoon, with sharply particled matter blowing upward; elegantly dressed pedestrians of both sexes hurry past him, bent slightly at the waist, as though to launch themselves into battle. He cannot read their eyes. And then Lizzie comes striding towards him, in a chocolate-colored linen dress with a cream silk jacket, carrying a red attaché case, her ash-colored hair flying back from her face.

Of course it is not the real Lizzie, his Lizzie, but another incarnation of her, Lizzie as she might look if her temperament inclined her to leveraged buy-outs rather than the Brontes. From the tilt of this other Lizzie's chin, her glinting geometric earrings, he deduces that she would not be shocked by what he has just agreed to. She would think it only sensible of him to sell out his hero and his principles to the highest, or only, bidder. But Lizzie would be shocked. Lizzie believes in art, and purity, and man's unconquerable mind.

On the D train heading for Brooklyn, restored to the world of the scruffy and shabby, he starts composing a letter to Sasha Borodin, a belated assertion of honor: "I must have been mad," it goes, "back there in your gallery. I must have been temporarily insane. That's what the art world does to painters in the 1980s." But on arriving home, instead of sitting down to write it, he phones Lizzie, even though the rates haven't gone down yet.

"Prokoff residence."

"Jesus, you sound like a servant. Don't let her turn you into a servant."

"Oh, it's you," she says happily, and then, as though registering the hour, "Is anything wrong?"

"Everything's fine. I just wanted to talk to you."

"You're still coming this weekend?"

"Of course I am."

"And you remember how to get to the house?"

"Of course. How are things going?"

"Fine," she says, in a wary voice, so that he knows she is not alone.

"Has that guy come back? The biographer?"

"Not yet."

"So what are you doing?"

"We're reading *Bleak House*."

"That sounds like a real snore."

"How's your painting going?"

"Like shit. I may be in this group show on Fifty-seventh Street. In a new gallery in the Fuller Building. It's not definite yet, but the woman really likes my work."

"Oh, but that's wonderful."

"Yeah . . . let's see."

"When did this happen?"

"Just today. I just got back from there." He sees Sasha Borodin in his mind's eye, with her tongue darting in and out of her thin lips. Not a terrier, he thinks, but a lizard. A fly-catcher.

"So that's why you phoned," Lizzie says delightedly.

"I guess. I guess I should go now. Call me soon, okay?"

"Of course I will."

"When you can talk."

Afterwards he tries, in a spirit of penance, to work; he even unrolls the painting that was based on Cézanne's mountains and looks it over, to make sure it still seems as good as when he painted it. But Sasha Borodin's praise has soured him on it in some insidious way; it looks self-conscious to him, too clever by half, like a campy in-joke instead of an homage.

She is likely to turn up at his studio, before the group show, and tell him she wants more like that, or more sensuous shapes, or lots of reds and greens and purples. However he tries, he cannot summon up the old joy at the thought of presenting his work to the world. It is impossible to think of Sasha Borodin and glory in the same breath. What he hungered for all those years, all his fantasies of being elevated and triumphant, have been reduced to the hope of hanging his work in an expensive gallery, under accurate lighting. For this he has made his Faustian bargain; this is the market value of his soul.

If Lizzie were there, she might quote Milton: 'That last infirmity of noble mind.' But Lizzie is out on Long Island, flushed with pleasure at his news, he is sure. And if she were there, he could never admit what he is thinking; he would have to pretend it was only mass and color and the fluidity of line he cared about, only radiance and immortality. The more corrupt he becomes, the more he will need to cultivate her image of him; all that will be left of his glory will be his reflection in her eyes. Poor Lizzie. But she has always seemed peculiarly suited to the role of vestal virgin. Besides, she is young: she can easily afford to waste a year or two before moving on.

He rolls up his canvas, splashes water on his face, and heads for Milo's.

17

"MAMA'S IN THE BASEMENT MIXIN' UP THE MEDICINE, I'm on the pavement thinking about the government . . . I don't want to work for Maggie's ma no more . . . Everybody says she's the brains behind Pa . . ." While he screws in the brackets for the railings, Sam Hazen is playing sixties songs on his boombox. First it was Jefferson Airplane, and now Bob Dylan is keening and wailing from a scratchy tape. Lizzie can't believe that Belle will permit such a thing in her house, but so far she hasn't uttered a word of protest.

This morning, after summoning Lizzie to bring her to the little table in the living room where the phone is kept, she sent them all into the garden while she made a call. This afternoon, she received a call in return and shooed them out again while she took it. Lizzie, however, returning to the house to fetch her sunglasses, heard her saying, "How the hell should I know? I haven't seen her in thirty-eight years."

Meanwhile Sam, who arrived not only with railings but a photograph of a carved Elizabethan chair torn from a book, is banging away cheerfully, whistling in time to his music. Late that afternoon, when yet another call comes and the three of them troop outside once more, he pulls a joint from his pocket and asks Lizzie if she'd like to smoke. Nina stares at the ground while Lizzie says politely that she wishes she could, but she really doesn't feel it would be right, not when she's supposed to be looking after Belle.

"Hey, maybe it'd be good for the old lady if you lightened up. Jesus, the uptightness around this house. You could cut it with a knife. She'd probably heal faster if the atmosphere was different."

"It's just that I have to be compos mentis in case she needs me for anything."

"Don't worry, my grass ain't that good. I only wish it was."

Just then Belle calls them back inside, and the subject is dropped. But when Sam and Nina are leaving, and Lizzie is in the kitchen heating up the stew for Belle's supper, he comes up behind her. "Go on, take it," he says, laying the joint on the counter. "Smoke it when she goes to bed."

"I can't, really," Lizzie says, conscious that he is standing uncomfortably close.

"You need something to make you smile. Am I making you uptight? I don't mean to. I just like you, that's all."

"I like you, too," she mumbles, willing him to go away. Instead, Nina enters, and then stops in the doorway. Lizzie feels herself turning red.

"Come on, get her to take this jay off me," Sam says. "She needs to loosen up a little."

"I don't want to," Lizzie stammers.

"Please, Sam," Nina says imploringly. He pockets the joint, shrugging, and leaves the room. Nina stays behind.

"You won't say anything, will you?"

"You mean to her? Of course not."

"She's so down on him."

"I'd never do that, honest," Lizzie says. Nina gives her a radiant smile and hurries out.

Belle, meanwhile, is in the living room, making her way doggedly, hand over hand, along the railings Sam has installed. Watching her from the doorway, Lizzie sees her put a hand to the small of her back and wince, but a minute later she continues her grim progress.

"Don't you think you've practiced enough for today?" Lizzie asks. "You're going to tire yourself out."

"I've got to practice. I'm preparing to go out."

"Where?"

"I don't know exactly. I don't know when either. But there's someone I have to see. An old friend. You can drive me, when I find out where we're going."

"Couldn't this person come to you?"

"I doubt it. She may not want to see me."

"Is it the lady with your journals?"

"Don't be presumptuous."

Later that evening, when they are playing another round of gin rummy, Belle asks, "Do you think Sam Hazen is on drugs?"

"What do you mean?"

"What do you mean, what do I mean? It's perfectly obvious. Do you think he's some sort of drug addict?"

Lizzie tells herself that smoking dope and being a drug addict are two entirely separate things, and Belle must mean heroin or something, which enables her to answer with conviction. "Definitely not."

Belle looks at her appraisingly. "But do you think he takes drugs?"

"Everybody takes drugs," Lizzie blurts out. "I mean, occasionally. Once in a while. He probably does, too."

"Then why can't he keep still?"

"I guess he's just nervous."

"Oh, really," Belle says. "That's ridiculous. What kind of drugs do you take?"

"Excuse me?"

"I'm curious. You said everybody did. That must include you."

"I've smoked marijuana."

"Tea, we used to call it. And what else? Cocaine? Ecstasy? LSD?"

"A little bit."

"Enough to tell if someone else is on drugs or not?"

"I don't know," Lizzie says miserably.

"You needn't sound so dramatic. I'm not about to turn him in

116

to the FBI. I'm going to bed now. I'll call you if I need you. Or come down if you hear a crash."

An hour later, as the sound of her snores ascends the stairs, Lizzie creeps down to the telephone. There is no door between her and Belle, she will not really feel free to talk, but she wants, at least, the comfort of hearing Paul's voice.

Cupping her hand around the receiver, she tells him the whole story in a jumble: about Sam, the joint, how Nina asked her not to tell, how Belle questioned her.

"He was trying to put the moves on you."

"Don't be silly," she says, though it felt like that to her, too. "Nina was in the next room."

"That doesn't mean anything. I'll have to straighten him out when I get there. What's the weather like? Is it sunny?"

"Sort of. Are you definitely coming?"

"Of course I am. On Friday."

"The only problem is, I might have to drive her someplace. To visit someone. I can't really talk about it right now."

"Are you saying I shouldn't come?"

"Of course not. I'm just hoping I won't have to take her on Friday. I can't wait to see you."

"Well, I can't wait either. I really want to meet the old girl properly. So I'll see you Friday, okay? And we can talk then."

"What's wrong with talking now?"

"It's a dead loss. You're whispering like you're in goddamn church. Besides, I'm working, and I'm worried the paint will dry on the palette. It's very expensive pigment. Cadmium red." But for once even this reference to his art cannot make her humble; the minute she hangs up, resentment floods in.

If the situation had been reversed, if he had been feeling low, what quantities of energy, love, intelligence she would have rallied to cheer him. She would have stayed on the phone for hours, gladly, until she was sure he was all right. She lies on the narrow bed of the guestroom with *Villette* unopened in her hands, remembering the time she was with him on Broadway, after he'd spent the night, and they ran into Heather, who came and had breakfast with them. Later, on the steps of Butler Library, Heather said, "You really coddle him, don't you? I guess guys his age expect that kind of thing from women."

"So where is your friend going to sleep?" Belle asks her the next morning. "The painter — what's his name again?"

"Paul. Paul Doherty."

"Paul Doherty. It won't be very comfortable, the two of you in that tiny bed in the guestroom, and I'm not sure I want you in my room. Together, that is. I think you'd better move into my room and give him yours."

"Thank you."

"You'll have to change the sheets on my bed. Nina will give you some fresh ones."

So for the first time Lizzie enters the bedroom, with its faint smell of liniment and its oak dresser where the photographs may or may not be. Certainly there are no pictures of Clay Madden in evidence, not even on the rickety cabinet that serves as a nighttable. Even the walls are bare, except for one painting next to the window, a small abstract in gray and green with BP in the corner.

And then there is the bed, an old, dark, high bed with four posts ending in carved pineapples, a shorter bed than any modern one, and not so wide either: clearly the place where Belle and Clay Madden slept together. She circles it respectfully for a minute before peeling back the old-fashioned blue blanket by its ribboned edge.

Sam appears in the doorway, his foot jerking up and down in its eternal staccato rhythm. "You need a hand?"

"No, I'm fine," she says, but he comes inside nonetheless and lifts the mattress so she can ease the bottom covering off. While she is struggling with the sheet, he leans across to help her, yanking it out from her side. Lizzie jumps.

"What's wrong with you, girl? Are you always this nervous?"

"I'm not nervous."

"Sure you are. I guess it's me. I guess I make you uncomfortable, huh? I don't mean to. I just like you, that's all."

118

Again, she tells him she likes him too, but this time she adds, "And I love Nina."

He laughs, drumming his fingers on the bedpost. "Sure you do. Nobody could not love Nina. You'd have to be the devil or something. You think I don't know that? You think I don't know she's better than I'm ever going to be? But sometimes I think I'm, like, Judas or something, you know what I mean? The one that's nailing her to the cross."

"I need to get some sheets," Lizzie says, sidling away.

"Sure you do. I'll get out if you want. You just got to tell me."

Lizzie flees.

Over lunch, Sam brings in a bottle of wine from his truck, and presses some even on Belle. "Come on, it will thicken your blood," he says, and winks. Then he tells her he has been checking out her land for her: it is full of wood alfalfa, which will do more for her arthritis, he says, than any pill. "It's an old Indian remedy; they knew what they were doing. Better than we do. They had a few things straight, those dudes." Just then the phone rings. Lizzie gets up to answer it, but Belle tells her to stay put. "Take me over there," she says peremptorily to Sam. Ignoring the arm she has stretched towards him, he lifts her, chair and all, and carries her into the hall over her objections.

When he returns, grinning, Lizzie pushes back her chair with the maximum amount of scraping and starts energetically gathering up the cutlery, clinking the forks together so that Belle can conduct her business in private. But she cannot help listening, too.

"I'm sure that's the one," Belle is saying. "Give me the address again . . . yes, and the phone number. Tell me exactly what they told you . . . Yes, that's fine. You can send me your bill."

A minute later she hobbles back to the kitchen.

"What's today?" she asks Lizzie.

"Thursday."

"I need you to drive me somewhere on Saturday." Lizzie does not point out that Paul will be there on Saturday, but Belle remembers. "You can bring your friend along if you like. I won't need you once I get there. The two of you can have some time alone together."

"Where are we going?" Lizzie asks, while Nina goes to fetch Belle's chair from the hallway.

"To Ardsley."

"But that's where you got married."

Belle makes a face. "I know perfectly well it's where I got married. What have we got for dessert?"

Later, she asks Lizzie to bring her into the living room, where she sits without speaking for a long time, watching through the window as a squirrel scurries up the trellis and races down again.

"Are you feeling all right?" Lizzie asks anxiously.

"Just tired," Belle says, but it isn't true. What she is really feeling, what has taken her by surprise, is a fierce elation at the thought of seeing Sophie again: her friend, her more than friend, a whole lost piece of her life could be restored to her, if only she can manage it. She will say, "I was crazy that day," or "You were right," something as simple as that.

"You always have to be right, don't you, you don't really care how many people die as long as you can be right": she had screamed those words at Sophie in the kitchen on Bank Street, the last time she ever saw her.

It was just after the war ended in Europe. The pictures of the camps had started appearing in the newspapers, and she was waking up screaming night after night. For once, Clay rallied himself and tried to comfort her, but she could not talk to Clay about it, or anyone else she knew on the Island. They had become the Other; she could not explain to them why she had to grieve and grieve for those piles of skeletons over in Poland, why it would be wrong to stop. She had to get to Sophie.

So she took the train into the city, on a sunny Wednesday morning, and knocked on Sophie's door.

But Sophie had refused to comfort her; Sophie had refused to say, even, that she couldn't have done anything even if she'd tried. "You want me to sit shiva with you, is that it? It's too late. Too late for you to come here crying. You knew it was happening, everyone knew. There were rallies, meetings, it was in the *Times* even. But when I tried talking to you about it, you didn't want to hear. Because it wasn't happening to him. Only his suffering counted."

"Shut up," Belle kept saying, "for God's sake, Sophie, shut up." But of course Sophie would not shut up.

"It's a moral disgrace, the way you're living. I'm not going to tell you it's okay."

She had grabbed her handbag and stormed out of there. All the way to Penn Station, as she plunged along through the crowds, she was thinking of things she should have said to Sophie, worse insults even than the ones she had yelled as she left. But she kept remembering, too, the painting that had hung over the kitchen table, clearly one of Sophie's, but darker than her work had been before the war, the shapes larger and more menacing. She had wanted to tell her that she liked that painting.

She still has dreams in which she meets Sophie on the street and Sophie turns away, unforgiving; and others, less frequent, in which everything is all right between them: they are talking, laughing, interrupting each other, under a sky as blue as Giotto's heaven. She remembers Sophie saying that, Jewish or not, she was going to ascend into a Fra Angelico when she died. She remembers hurrying towards Bank Street at midnight, because there was something she had to tell Sophie before she could sleep — a revelation about suffering, news of a breakthrough with her painting. At the time, she had never thought of it as love. Love was something different, more painful, reserved exclusively for men. Now she would rather have Sophie back than any of them. If Sophie will permit it, maybe she can tell her that too.

18

"YOU KNOW WHAT I WANT?" MARNIE SAYS.

Nothing could interest him less, she knows that, but the point is long past when she might have stopped herself from telling him. The hunger is upon her, her words, her touch, are all suffused with it. Blindly, her fingers reach out now for Mark Dudley, crawl over him, while he lies there silent, refusing to give her what she needs.

Nor has she done much better by him; she has obdurately refused to be drawn out about the car crash, which explains, perhaps, why he has retreated into chilly dislike.

"I want a big old house in the country, with lots of animals. Chestnut horses. Big furry dogs. An apple orchard. And a huge stone fireplace. I don't think I'd care if I never saw a human being again. Even when I was a kid I felt that way. There were eight of us, I had to share a room with two of my sisters, and I'd think, 'Some day I'll have a house all to myself, and I won't even let anyone else in it.'"

Yawning deliberately, he removes one hand from under his head and scratches his balls. Then, still without touching her, he returns it to its former place. She sighs, propping herself up on one elbow.

"He had horses, you know, when he was a kid. He used to tell me stories about them." He stirs slightly, but still says nothing. "Do you want to hear about his horses?"

"Not particularly."

"I can't talk about that night, I can't."

He turns to face her at last. "Then tell me about Belle Prokoff."

"What do you mean? Tell you what about her?"

"He had to have talked to you about her. Complained or explained or something. You must have asked about her, it's the normal thing to do. Girlfriends do ask about wives, don't they? At least in my experience."

"What are you trying to tell me? That you're married?"

"Not at the moment, no. It was just a general observation."

"I don't see why you have to be so snide about everything."

"It's just a way I have. So tell me what he said about Belle Prokoff."

"He didn't . . . we didn't talk about all that. He used to say some time we'd be together, and I didn't pressure him for more. I was very young, I just accepted that it would all work out somehow."

"I thought he'd taken you out there once, to the house. When she was still living there."

"Oh God, who told you about that?"

"Someone I interviewed. And it came up at the inquest after his death, remember?"

"No, I don't . . . what does that have to do with the accident, anyway?"

"I don't know, but it was entered into the transcript."

"If you've read the transcript, then you know more than I do. I can't remember back that far."

"Just try. What happened when he took you to the house? Did he introduce you? Did he say, 'This is my wife Belle'? Or what? He must have said something before you went there."

She flops down, burying her head in the pillow. "He said, 'I want you to see my studio. We'll just go in there and get right out again.'"

"I can't hear you."

She turns her head a little. "I said, he told me we'd go to the studio for a minute and then get out of there. So that's what we did."

"He didn't say, 'My wife is there'? Come on. He must have told you something about her in all that time."

"He told me he felt sorry for her, things were very bad between them and she didn't really have anyone else. He told me he couldn't desert her, that he always intended to look after her no matter what happened. But he wanted to be with me, he wanted us to live together, that was the important thing. All right?"

"All right. So he took you to the studio, and then what?"

"Then . . . we looked at the paintings he'd been working on. There was one he said was for me; it had a lot of purple in it, and gray, and these fine traces of orange, like lacework. God, it was beautiful. He said it was mine because he'd been thinking of me when he did it, whatever happened to him he wanted me to have it. Only of course she wouldn't give it to me, not even when I got other people to ask her for it. But I'll remember that painting forever. It's mine. She never sold it, I think she was afraid there'd be publicity if she did. It's probably sitting in a vault somewhere."

"I thought he wasn't painting anymore by then."

"That's not what he said. He showed me stuff he was working on, and then when he died they dated them all earlier, like he hadn't been painting, but I don't know. I think he was. Some of them were rolled up in a corner, I remember that, and he unrolled them for me. And that was that. We got back into the car and left."

"You're sure about that?"

"Of course I'm sure."

"At the inquest it was noted that Belle Prokoff had called the police and told them to throw you off her property."

"You bastard."

"I guess you forgot that part, is that right?"

"You fucking bastard."

The policeman had been too embarrassed even to look at her; he rubbed his chin and looked out over the marshes while mumbling that he was sure she was a reasonable girl, he was sure she wouldn't want to stay where she wasn't wanted. Meanwhile Clay was shouting, "It's my house, I can bring whoever I want." Like a teenage son, like a little boy. And Belle, standing on the front porch, stared at her with such contempt she felt shriveled inside. Belle was in a shapeless brown dress and an old cardigan with leather buttons like a man's, a kerchief tied tight over her head. She was shocked at how old Belle looked, and ugly. In her flowered skirt and lacy white blouse, with her nails freshly painted, her blond hair smoothed into a shining pageboy, she felt as though she were the one with all the weapons on her side, and was ashamed for the first time. No one could have convinced her back then that it wasn't enough, being pretty, that some day she would find herself envying Belle Prokoff, whose cardigan had struck such horror into her heart.

Mark Dudley is looking at her speculatively, smiling in a way she does not like. "What is it?" she says, sitting up. "What are you thinking?"

"About you and him," he says, stroking her lightly between the breasts. "Shall I tell you about that?"

"What do you mean?"

"I mean I've finally figured out what the real story was. Do you want to hear it?"

"I don't know," she says, shrinking away. She pulls the sheet over herself, to cover her breasts. "I'm not sure."

"Of course you do." He lies back down without touching her, his hands folded again beneath his head. "There's this guy, see, he's in his forties, and he's this great painter, everyone says so, only he can't seem to paint much anymore. Can't paint at all, in fact. And everyone knows that, too, they're half waiting for him to do something great again and half hoping he'll fall on his face. He can see it in their eyes, how they don't wish him well, they want him to fail, to come down to their level, and he can't let himself do that, he's got to prove they're wrong."

"It wasn't like that," she says, but he shushes her.

"And then he meets this beautiful Irish bird, really young and lush, see, with aquamarine eyes, and she worships him. She doesn't know he's all washed up, or afraid he is. She thinks he's a god. And he starts seeing things through her eyes, he starts feeling like a big shot again, for a little while anyway. She'll do anything he wants, in bed or out, and he hopes maybe that will charge his batteries again, only it doesn't work. Fucking her doesn't mean he can paint again. So he starts abusing her a little, maybe slapping her around, insulting her, just because she hasn't really helped him, or because she doesn't even get it — she doesn't know he's a washout — and he despises her for that."

"That's crazy," she says, "you're getting it all wrong." She is thinking of how it really was, how he sat in her room with the velvet curtains, crying, and she would get up from the window seat to comfort him, to stroke his back, his head, his shoulders, whisper that it was all right. She loved him because he was the only man she could imagine crying like that in front of her without being ashamed.

"It wasn't much, your grand love affair, it wasn't such a torrid romance after all, was it? You were more for show than anything else. Because he was drunk all the time, and everyone knows drunks aren't really interested in sex. They can't get it up, or they pass out in the middle, or puke all over the sheets. Right? Isn't that what really happened?"

"No. It was nothing like that."

"You've been living on it for how many years now?"

What amazes her is not his nastiness — she has never supposed him to be kind — but that he could so drastically misunderstand. What she'd been in love with was the pain that Clay Madden carried around with him; she had opened her arms to it, and he'd come crawling in. A man she slept with just once, a Frenchman she'd met in a hotel bar, said to her over breakfast, "You have a gift for sadness," and she knew he was right. She did not even have a gift for sex, she had a gift for sadness.

What kind of life can Dudley have had if the only secrets he is capable of imagining are ugly ones? She wants to tell him what it was like for her after Clay Madden died, all the men who wanted to sleep with her because of him. And then the first man it didn't make her feel sick to go to bed with she had married, the first man who watched her cry without trying to jolly her out of it.

"Tell me about that night in the car," Mark Dudley says. "Come on. I want to know."

His tone is commanding, bullying, but she is looking at his penis, lolling on the sheet in a sickle shape, so it seems impossible it could ever be erect. His balls, too, look rosy and defenseless, so sweet and harmless, in contrast to his voice, that she starts to laugh. Pretty soon she is helpless with laughter, thinking of the German woman who answered Stuart Hollis' phone, and Belle Prokoff's cardigan, and her own unappeasable hunger, all of them equally absurd. The tears flow down her cheeks; she clutches her sides, gasping, cannot let herself stop, not even when he shouts and curses her, not even when he rises from the bed and starts putting on his clothes.

She has to keep it up because otherwise she may tell him what he wants to know. In exchange for the next drink, the next kiss, the next fuck, she might still weaken. But she is almost safe. He is stomping around the room, snatching up his socks, his shoes, his wallet. He will be gone soon, and then, finally, she can stop laughing.

What Clay Madden said to her that night was simply "Fuck it," over and over and over again. "Fuck it, fuck them, I've had it": those were the last, enraged words that she omitted to mention at the inquest. They did not seem to add stature to his death. She hears Mark Dudley slam the front door behind him, and shudders once, and stops: she has won. If she has to be a whore, at least she can manage never to be a success at it.

19

LIZZIE CAN HARDLY BELIEVE THAT PAUL IS FINALLY THERE, in Belle's living room, that she has been the agent of bringing these two together. For the past half hour now, she has been in a state of painful agitation, half proud and half alarmed every time they open their mouths. They are too blunt and irascible, too nakedly, embarrassingly themselves, to be entirely safe. Wishy-washy though she is in comparison, she is more supple than they are, less vulnerable to the dangers of exposure.

"And then I had this graduate student who'd never seen a Cézanne," Paul is saying. "And when I told her she shouldn't be studying painting if she didn't know Cézanne, she reported me for sexual harassment. Can you imagine that? Can you imagine Cézanne getting a fucking M.F.A.? The world's gone barking mad."

"The world's always been mad."

"Not like this. At least you got to be part of something that was real, it wasn't all hype back then. I bet you didn't meet a single painter who couldn't talk about Cézanne."

"You needn't envy me. I can't paint anymore. I can't move my hands. Try that one for a while."

It is a beautiful, golden day, the air shimmering with sunlight. "You should get Lizzie to take you into the garden," Belle says.

"You come with us."

"I can't risk it. The ground's too uneven."

"Sure you can. You just hold on to me, I'll look after you."

Pretty soon he has hoisted her up and she is leaning on his arm, walking painfully towards the back door. "That's right," he says encouragingly, stooping to accommodate her. "Well done. Careful of that raised bit, now. Okay, when you step onto the grass, make sure to put your heel down all the way."

Just outside the door Belle turns to Lizzie, hovering solicitously behind them. "Go get some deckchairs out of the shed. There should be four in there." Paul looks from one to the other of them, beaming. When Lizzie returns with the chairs, he first ensconces Belle in one and then arranges another for Lizzie, fussing with it until he is sure she won't have the sun in her eyes. Lizzie can hardly remember being so happy.

"Do you need a hat?" Paul asks Belle, taking a chair for himself.

"Of course not."

"It's beautiful here," he says, his eyes lingering on the studio.

"The town wants me to give them this place, did you know that? Leave it to them in my will."

"What do they want it for?"

"Preserve it. Keep it open. So people can come and look. But they don't have the money; they want that too."

"And you don't want to give it to them?"

"I'm not going to sell Maddens," she says shortly, "so they can get themselves a museum."

He is silent for a moment. "So you won't do it?"

"There's enough money out here now so they can raise the funds if they really want to. If enough people are interested. You see those red flowers there? Next to the lilies? They're from Australia, too."

"They're probably much happier here."

Just then a wasp comes and settles on her face, and when she brushes it away it stings her hand; her good mood is ruined. They escort her back inside, where Lizzie goes to fetch something for the swelling. "Don't keep fussing over me," Belle grumbles. "You go back outside, and I'll try to take a nap. I want to feel rested tomorrow." She turns to Paul. "We're going on an excursion together, did she tell you? A journey in search of my past."

Lizzie decides to take Paul to the bay, where they can be alone together, but just as they are leaving the house, Sam drives up in his rusted pickup and rolls down the window, tooting his horn.

"Hello there, Lizzie girl. Hello there, Lizzie's old man. Where are you two headed?"

"To the bay."

"Don't do that, it'll be crowded with ladies with kids. You want me to take you someplace special?"

"That's all right," Lizzie says.

"Come on, I might as well. Hop in. I'll show you the secret places. You got decent shoes on?" Already, Paul is opening the truck door; Lizzie slides in next to Sam, and then they are off, gravel flying up all around them.

"So you're a painter," Sam says, accelerating onto the road.

"That's right."

"You paint this kind of stuff?" He gestures grandly at the landscape. "Sea views and all that?"

"Not any more."

"I guess nobody does it anymore, right? Not the highbrow types. Beats me why not. You think nature's got nothing to teach you?"

"Of course it's got things to teach me. But that doesn't mean I have to paint it."

"If I was a painter I'd paint one tree over and over my whole life. I even know which tree. You want to see it? It's not that far from here."

"We can't," Lizzie says. "She's just taking a nap, she might wake up any time."

"You and Nina. She's got you right under her thumb, right in harness. And does she ever love it."

"You don't like her?" Paul asks.

"I think she's great, I love the old lady. But you can't let her start bullying you, or she'll never stop. You can see why he fucked around."

"Who?"

"Madden. Had himself a girl on the side."

"Everyone knows that," Paul says. "But you couldn't have known him yourself. You're too young."

"I was five and a half when he died. But I still remember him. My dad had a body shop, see, and Madden used to come by and mess with the welding tools. He liked me for some reason, he always told my dad he didn't treat me right. Didn't appreciate what a great kid I was. And sometimes he took me places in his car. To the beach and stuff. Plus he gave me my first dog."

"No shit."

"Yeah. It was a stray he'd picked up down in the cove, a collie type mutt, and his other dog got jealous, see. So he brought it down to the shop and managed to talk my dad into letting me keep it. Shit, that dog was smart. I cried like a baby when it died."

"What else do you remember about him?"

"You one of those Clay Madden freaks? There's some old guys out here, they go into their Madden riffs every year for the summer people, get them to buy 'em a beer."

"I'll buy you two beers if you tell me more stories."

"He your hero or something?"

"Yeah. My number one hero. And I've just been sitting in his garden with his widow, and now I'm driving in a pickup truck with a guy he gave his first dog to. You can take the piss out of me all you want, mate, I'm feeling pretty good."

"This place I'm taking you to," Sam says after a pause, "he was the one who showed it to me. He told me it was a special place. After he died I went looking for it, but I couldn't find it again, until one day I was twelve or something, I was playing Indians with some of my buddies. We were tracking a deer, and then we came into this clearing. I knew right away where I was. It has a feel to it. You can say a prayer for his soul when we get there, okay?"

He veers abruptly off the road, onto a narrow dirt track. Branches scrape at the windshield, dust flies up everywhere. Sam laughs out loud, pounding the dashboard. "Hang onto your hats," he says as the truck plunges down an incline, wobbles on three wheels, and bumps its way right to a stand of trees. A minute later, it comes to a halt.

"Okay, this is where we get out, ladies and gentlemen. This is where civilization ends and the animals take over."

He and Paul jump out, leaving Lizzie to fend for herself. By the time she has lowered herself carefully from the truck, stumbled over a bush, and righted herself, they are striding off into the woods.

"You see that plant over there? That's wood alfalfa. I was telling Mrs. Madden, the Indians used it to cure arthritis. You know anything about that?"

"I don't know the first thing about plants."

"You ought to learn. You could make your own colors, like artists used to."

"Some time maybe I will."

"If I was a painter I'd mix everything from scratch. And use egg whites for binder."

Lizzie, panting slightly, has caught up with them in a stand of trees. The farther she gets into the woods, the colder it is, and darker. She is not at all sure she likes it. But then the light changes; they are in a sunny grove, full of blue and red wildflowers; a dozen white butterflies rise up as they walk.

"Okay," Sam says. "Here it is. The special spot. And that's the tree." He points to a huge old maple on the other side that towers over the stunted trees around it. "We can lie underneath it like he probably did, and maybe smoke a little weed and watch the sky. Come on, Liz. You sit on this moss here, it's the softest place."

"I'm just afraid I won't be there when she wakes up."

"So Nina will be there. Nina can look after her fine. I don't want to get back when she's asleep, anyway. I need to show her the drawings for her chair."

"What chair?" Paul asks, and Sam describes the larch and cherrywood throne he's designed to carry Belle up and down the stairs.

"I've been doing some research on cables for it. They got these lightweight plastics now that are stronger than metal."

Paul says it really is amazing, the resin compounds they make these days. Lizzie is thinking how cheerful men seem when they're together, and what boring things they talk about, when Sam jumps up.

"You want to climb this mother?"

"I haven't climbed a tree in thirty years."

"Come on. He would have. Right to the top. That's the thing they don't get about him, not really. He was a wild man. He wouldn't have sat around talking to them about art. Let's do it."

"All right, you've talked me into it."

"Great." Sam turns to Lizzie, who is just about to protest. "Don't worry, I'll look after him for you." And he is as good as his word. Watching them from below, Lizzie sees him bounce on a branch to test its strength before waving Paul on. Meanwhile Paul is whooping with delight. "It's wonderful," he calls down to her. "It's wonderful up here." Finally, he arrives at the top branch and balances there, silhouetted against the sun, his hair and beard glinting as he turns his face upwards. Lizzie knows she will remember him like that forever.

"Thank you," Paul says solemnly, when they are down again and heading for the truck. He squeezes Sam's shoulder. "Thank you for making me climb Madden's tree."

"It's okay, man," Sam says, and winks at Lizzie, who up until then was almost liking him. Now she looks uneasily at Paul, wanting to warn him.

Later, back at the house, when Paul is talking to Belle, Sam comes up behind her in the kitchen. "I like your artist, he's a great guy. Pretty intense. He's got to learn to laugh at himself. But you're sure crazy about him, aren't you? I can see that." He lays a folded square of tin foil down on the counter. "I told him I'd give him this, but he's in with the old lady, so you give it to him, okay? Take some tonight, go ahead. Have yourselves a ball," he says, and laughs out loud.

20

"HOW ARE YOU, SOPHIE?"

"As you see."

"Aren't you going to ask me to sit down?"

But Sophie only shrugs.

"I've got to sit, Sophie, I can't walk very well."

"Then go ahead and sit. I can't stop you."

On the whole length of the porch, there is neither a vacant chair nor any attendant in sight. But a fat, red-faced blonde is seated nearby, staring sullenly at the golf course, while at her side a withered female dressed in a track suit, like Sophie (hers is green today, the other woman's pink), fumbles for the bright liquid on the tray of her wheelchair. I would rather die, Belle thinks, than wind up like that. I have got to find a way to die.

"Could you help me for a minute?" she asks the blonde, who looks at her blankly. "I have to sit down," Belle says, angry now. "Do you think you could find me a chair?"

With a twitch of her shoulders, the woman rises to her feet and heads inside, wobbling on her high heels. A minute later she returns with a battered plastic chair, which she sets downs with a bang just far enough from Sophie so that they will have to shout.

"Thank you," Belle says, and seats herself gingerly, fearful of falling off.

"Could you move a little closer?" she asks Sophie.

"You're used to giving orders, I can see that."

"It's just that yours has wheels and mine doesn't."

Grunting, Sophie presses a lever on her right and one on her left, and scuttles a few inches closer. For a moment they stare at each other. Belle notes the map of wrinkles on her friend's face and has the unworthy thought that Sophie looks older than she does.

"You haven't changed much," she says in atonement. "I still would have known you."

"I would have known you too. But I've seen your picture in the papers."

Again there is silence.

"I've thought about you a lot. I've dreamed about you."

"Maybe. But you didn't come. When that man asked me about the journals, I thought, Now it will happen, she'll come. It wasn't an accident."

"I didn't know where you were."

"Don't make excuses."

"You could have gotten in touch with me if you wanted."

"It wasn't my place to do that. You were the one who left in a huff."

"Because you insulted me. You said it was a disgrace, how I was living. You said I was worse than the goyim." And suddenly they are glaring at each other in exactly the old way. The names Sophie called her in June 1945 are fresh in Belle's mind, just as Sophie, she knows, is remembering her sins of the war years and finding them unforgivable all over again. They could spend this whole reunion refighting that last fight.

It is Sophie who speaks first. "So you got what you wanted," she says. "He's the famous genius, just like you always said."

"Don't you ever forgive anyone?"

"What, because I'm old I'm supposed to be filled with benevolence? The world gets worse and worse, but I'm not supposed to notice?"

"I'm not the world, Sophie, don't take it out on me. I'm an old woman. You could go a little easy."

"I'm doing my best, believe me. How did you get here, anyway?"

"Someone drove me."

"And you told them to come back in half an hour? An hour? How long did you figure it would take to get those books from me?"

"God, Sophie, I thought I was bitter."

"If it had been me, I would have found you somehow. I would have said I was sorry forty years ago."

"You never said you were sorry for anything."

"Didn't I? I'm sorry about a lot of things. Sorry I wound up like this, in this place. Sorry I never had a child. Sorry for things I said to Howard, that I can't take back."

"I bought the book of his poems."

"Yes? That must have accounted for ten percent of sales."

"It got a nice notice in the *Times*."

"Don't be patronizing. It was one little paragraph. In a discussion of six books. Not a real review."

"Still, the man liked it."

"He singled out all the wrong ones for praise. The early ones, from before the war even. The later stuff was much better."

"They always get it wrong like that."

"And what about my work? What's going to happen to that?"

"Who's got it now?"

"It's in storage, mostly. In Yonkers. Except for some lithographs that a woman on Broome Street tries to sell for me. And when I die my niece will choose one picture for her living room and throw the rest out. That's where it will end up, in the dump."

"I'd like to see it."

"Yes? What for? When I thought about you coming, I thought, I'll make her get me a show somewhere, that's what I'll ask in return for the journals. I'll make a deal with my famous friend. That's what life is about nowadays, they tell me. Deals."

"You don't have to make a deal, Sophie. I'll see what I can do."

"You knew I'd give you the journals anyway. I don't care for that man, he's too agreeable."

"He's a lot worse than just agreeable."

"Maybe. But a weakling, anyone can see that. I don't think you should worry too much about him."

"What should I worry about, then?"

"Aren't you happy, *Sheine*?"

"Of course I'm not happy."

"Not even a little bit? It must be nice, after all, being rich and famous. Having people court you. A little bit nice, anyway. It must take the indignity out of old age."

"I can't paint anymore, my hands are so twisted. I can hardly do up my buttons."

"Well, I can't paint either, but nobody is courting me. You won't admit it's nice because then I might be jealous, is that it? You have to pretend we're in the same boat, that's the safe thing. But I'd like to know how it feels. The older I get, the more I want to know what other people feel, and the less they'll tell me. Nobody tells you the truth when you're old, that's the worst of all."

"They lie to me too. They tell me how much they love my paintings, when it's his they want. That's what it's like."

"They say you'd left him for good that summer he died."

"Do they?"

"Is it true?"

"I didn't know what I was going to do, I went away to try and decide. It was Ernest who made me do it. You remember Ernest."

"Sure. But he couldn't have made you if you didn't want to. Nobody ever made you do anything you didn't want."

"No. But he came to the house one day and yelled at me for still being there. And he quoted a poem to me, the same one Howard quoted the first time I ever met him. Do you remember it? About hearts that turned to stone."

"Too long a sacrifice/Can make a stone of the heart."

"That's the one."

"Only it wasn't that bit Howard loved. It was the bit about writing it out in a verse. And the terrible beauty."

"Well, it was what Ernest quoted that day."

"So you went away to think."

"That's right."

"And then he died. When they told me I thought, now she'll always blame herself. She'll think she killed him by going. But you would have thought that anyway."

"Of course."

"It's a terrible thing about the dead, how they can't comfort us but they go on accusing."

"But we accuse them, too."

"Listen to me. I want to get out of this place one last time. Could you do that for me?"

"Of course I could. I will. Next week, if you want."

"It's not so easy with a wheelchair."

"I can arrange it. I can rent a special car or something, and a driver. Whatever it takes. That's the good thing about having money. Where do you want to go?"

"I haven't gotten that far yet. I've just thought about getting out. Being back on a street somewhere, watching the people. But not the city, I don't think I could stand to go back to the Village now. So where could we go? White Plains? That's not a real place. Somewhere like Buffalo, a medium-sized dingy kind of place where nobody knows me. That's what I had in mind. But it doesn't make much sense, does it? It's like a kid thinking of running away."

"We can go to Buffalo if you want."

"No. It's crazy."

"I could take you out to the Island, then. You could stay with me for a few days. Only there wouldn't be so many people to watch. Just the summer people downtown."

"You've got someone that helps you? Who could get me in and out of this thing?"

"Yes."

"I could see your paintings."

"We could go get yours, too, if you wanted. From Yonkers. And bring some out. That way I'd have them there to show people."

"Okay," Sophie says. "And now do you want the journals?"

"You don't have to give them to me. Just don't give them to him. I thought you might have already."

"I let him see a couple, that's all. I wouldn't let him take them away. But you should take them, they belong to you."

"I don't even know if I want them."

"It might not be so good for you to read them."

"They're that bad?"

"They'll remind you of being unhappy."

"I remember bringing them over to your house one time, and the Italian women leaning out their windows on Bleecker, calling to each other. I still thought if I wanted to I could be like them, I could marry the man at North Pole Meats and have his children, and they'd talk to me, too."

"You always thought that: You could marry a stevedore, you could be a dress designer, or a call girl, you could still decide to be someone different when you grew up. You thought it was a fluke, you being who you were."

"And you always told me it wasn't true."

"I was right."

"I'm sorry, Sophie."

"It's okay. You're here now, I'm glad. When you go away I might get mad again, but right now it's okay. It's fine."

"When do you want to come see me?"

"You tell me."

"It doesn't matter."

"To me either."

"Say next Wednesday, then. I'll come pick you up at noon."

"You'll have to sign me out. Sign some papers."

"I could do it now."

"No, let me talk to them. I'll tell them you'll be responsible for me, I'll sign a paper saying so. Releasing them from responsibility. They won't care, then. The doctor will let me go, he's a little bit of a *mensch*, that doctor. Just a little, but enough."

"It doesn't look like such a bad place."

"It's the people. I don't like old people." She laughs. "Maybe we should say good-bye now, before my niece turns up. I think I'd better take a nap before she comes. All this excitement."

"Okay," Belle says, and realizes that she, too, is exhausted; she can hardly imagine standing up. She gropes for her stick, hung over the chairback, and forces herself to her feet. I am going to fall, she thinks, right here on the veranda, while that blond woman sits there gloating. I am going to fall down those steps and break my neck. But she does not fall, she does not die. She hobbles painfully down the steps, her cane trembling ahead of her, and there at the bottom are Paul and Lizzie, hovering a little ways away on the broad lawn that stretches to the edge of the golf course, looking inordinately flushed and peaceful, so that she knows they have been in a field somewhere, or the back seat of the car, or some other unlikely place, making love.

21

IN THE GRUNGIEST OF THE LOCAL HANGOUTS, A DIM
roadside bar with cracked linoleum and an ancient jukebox, Sam
has been watching Belle's nemesis work the crowd. First, Dudley
explained to the bartender that he was searching for the truth about
Clay Madden's death. Then he appealed for help to the men watching a golf tournament on the television: had any of them known
Madden personally? Could they shed any light on the events of his
final summer? Brian Rogers, who once did odd jobs for the Maddens'
neighbor, is now drinking Jack Daniels instead of his usual Molson,
a fact that seems to discomfit as much as please him. Sam suspects
his reminiscences are being fabricated for the occasion. "I told her
straight out she was in over her head, she ought to pack up and go
home," he says, speaking of Marnie Ryan.

"Do you remember what her answer was?"

"Not the words exactly," Rogers says. "But she didn't look too
happy, I remember that much." He keeps his head down, rolling
his glass around in his hand.

"Did you get the impression that he was in love with her?"
Dudley asks, and Rogers shifts uncomfortably in his seat. His real
impression of Clay Madden was that he was crazy as a bedbug; he
never considered it his business to contemplate the man's deeper
feelings.

"How about Mrs. Madden? Do you know her?"

"A little."

"So you know she can be a difficult woman."

Rogers looks at him uncertainly.

"Clay Madden gave his girlfriend a painting before he died, and Mrs. Madden refused to hand it over. Did you know that?"

Again, Rogers seems unsure what reaction is expected of him; maybe it doesn't seem unreasonable to him that under those circumstances a wife would hold a grudge.

"She's still hoping to get it some day," Dudley goes on. "She could certainly use the money, I'll tell you that much."

Before the other man can respond, Sam leans across the bar into Dudley's line of vision. "She'd like to talk to you," he says. "Mrs. Madden. When can you come see her?"

Dudley looks him up and down. "Is she a friend of yours?"

"You might say that."

"And she told you she wanted to see me?"

"Her exact words."

"Then tell me when to come, and I'll be there."

"How about tomorrow? Sunday. That sound good to you?"

"What time?"

"I'll check that out with her and let you know. Can I phone you some place later?"

"I'm at the Windjammer. Do you have the number?"

"I got a phone book," Sam says, sliding off his stool. "I'll look it up." He throws some money on the bar and saunters out, arms nice and loose at his sides. All the way to Belle's, he replays the scene in his head, cackling with delight.

Thirty miles to the north, Belle is snoring in the back seat while Lizzie and Paul, in front, exchange fond smiles, like doting parents. Finding nobody at home, Sam lets himself in with the key Nina hides under the eaves and listens intently to the silence. Occasionally, alone in the house like this, he can get a sense of Clay Madden's presence, impossible to feel when Belle is around. He sometimes thinks he wants Madden back more than she does; it's easier for her with him dead, less trouble, whereas he can't stop imagining all the talks they could have had, and the adventures, as he was growing up. Even his dad might have been nicer to him if Madden had stuck around. And Belle couldn't have treated him like some kind of servant.

Whistling defiantly, he takes the stairs two at a time and enters her bedroom, where he stands looking around him, hoping for inspiration. But he knows from past experience that the wardrobe holds only a few shapeless dresses and some depressing shoes, the drawers contain nothing but ace bandages and Dr. Scholl's corn plasters and bras that resemble trusses.

He heads for the guestroom, ignoring Paul's workshirt and balled-up socks on the floor, and fumbles half-heartedly through the dresser containing Lizzie's clothing. He checks out her bra size (34B) and the fiber content of some flowered underpants before coming across a beige plastic diaphragm case. In his opinion, she is definitely wasting herself on her painter, who's too wrapped up in his own head to appreciate her. He wishes he could bring her to her senses somehow.

Finally he clatters downstairs again, to rummage through the cubbyholes in the rolltop desk, but there is nothing of interest there either — only homeowner's policies, property tax notices, innumerable gas bills marked Paid, and a stained penny postcard, brown with age, sitting in lonely splendor in a tiny slot. He tries to read the message on the back, but it's faded almost to nothingness.

By the time the three travelers return, he is seated at the kitchen table, whistling the chorus from "Pinball Wizard."

Belle is leaning on Paul's arm; Lizzie, carrying her stick, brings up the rear. "Hello there," Sam says breezily, but Belle only grunts. He winks at Lizzie. "Your Englishman's back in town."

Belle grabs hold of a chair and sinks down, shaking off Paul's arm. "Have you spoken to him?"

"Uh-huh. He's a real smoothie, isn't he?"

"You told him I wanted to see him?"

"He'll come tomorrow if you want. I'm supposed to let him know what time."

"Tell him noon."

"Noon it is." He stands up, ready to leave, but Belle detains him.

"When can you have that chair ready?"

"Some time this week be good enough?"

"I need to move upstairs by Wednesday. A friend of mine is going to use the downstairs room."

"*No problema.* I'll get to work on the gliders tomorrow. Nina was coming over anyway, there's some meat she thinks you should use up." He looks at Paul. "Want to go to Carl's and see if Dudley's still there?"

Hardly ten minutes ago, as Belle groaned in her sleep, Paul had asked Lizzie to come to the beach with him and watch the sun set over the water. It was his last night, he'd said, stroking her hair; surely she could leave Belle alone for an hour after supper. And of course she said Yes, imagining them together on the dunes, with the waves turning pink and gold.

Now he gives her a quick, furtive look before telling Sam sure he'll come with him, why not.

"What about the sunset?" she bursts out. Sam grins at her, and she suddenly thinks of Iago and Edmund, all those villains in literature euphoric with their own malice.

"I'll be back in plenty of time," Paul says, avoiding her eyes.

"Do you promise?" She doesn't even care if she is making a fool of herself; she's doing it for the sake of his soul.

"Sure." He edges towards the door, still without looking at her.

"The classic sound," Belle says drily as they exit.

"What is?"

"A door slamming."

"You mean as a metaphor?"

"No. As a thing unto itself."

"I think Sam is evil," Lizzie says in a rush.

"He's no more evil than a lot of other people. He's just interfering with your plans at the moment. Anyway, it's your friend who's letting him do it, it's no good blaming Sam. Believe me."

But the last thing Lizzie wants is for Belle to turn against Paul. "It's because of your husband," she says.

"What are you talking about?"

"Because Sam knew your husband."

"That's nonsense. He must have been about two years old when he died."

"He was five and a half. Your husband gave him his first dog."

"He did not," Belle says, exasperated, and then stops. "Oh my God. That dog. I remember now. He gave it to some little boy whose father fixed his car. Was that Sam?"

"Yes."

"Well, that still doesn't explain why your friend went off like that. They've gone drinking. Or to take drugs."

It's the last thing that Lizzie wants to hear. "It'll be all right," she says brightly.

"Will it?"

"Of course it will. In the end."

"It's one thing to go ahead with it, it's another to pretend that everything's dandy."

Lizzie thinks this over. "If it won't ever be all right," she says finally, "then why go ahead with it at all?"

"Because," Belle says. "Because there's some other reason. One you find compelling at the time. It doesn't have to involve a happy ending. Where did you get this idea that everything comes out right in the end?"

"You have to have faith," Lizzie says, annoyed. "Don't you?"

"Not necessarily. "

"But you're supposed to, you're not supposed to let yourself despair."

"Your mother didn't have a very happy ending, did she? Wasn't that what you told me?"

"Yes."

"So how do you explain that?"

"I don't want to talk about it."

"Fine. We won't talk about it. Make us some dinner, and we'll both pretend that everything's fine."

Lizzie sets about heating Nina's chowder and slicing Nina's bread.

"You want me to be a fatalist," she says reproachfully, stirring the shimmering yellow soup.

"No, I don't."

"But you're saying there's nothing I can do, it'll never be all right."

"That's not what I meant at all."

"Then what are you telling me?"

"You can always decide to walk away. Get out of the whole mess while you can."

This is more hurtful to Lizzie than anything. Belle, who is famous for sticking it out, for enduring heroically for love's sake, assumes that Lizzie can just walk blithely away. She must not consider her worthy of suffering.

Lizzie lets the spoon drop and turns to face her.

"You didn't get out."

"No, I didn't," Belle says, her jaw thrust forward at exactly the angle of her self-portrait.

Lizzie looks at her for a moment in bafflement, until an awful thought enters her head. "Are you saying you should have?" she asks, her voice rising to a wail.

"I'm not saying anything. I'm just naming the possibilities. How long can it take to heat up some soup, for God's sake?"

After that she becomes very bossy, ordering Lizzie around: she ought to be using the flowered bowls, not the blue ones, and the spoons from the bottom drawer; she never cleans the place mats properly. Then, when they have finished their chowder, she catches Lizzie looking at the clock and says, "Get a pencil and paper. I want you to make a list."

"Of what?"

"Of the things we need to do before Sophie comes. Go on, get some paper."

"Just tell me. I'll remember."

"I want it written down."

Lizzie returns with her notebook and a felt-tipped pen.

"First of all," Belle says, "you have to buy soap."

"You've got lots of soap."

"We need fancy soap with little ribbons around it. And crinkled paper. The kind that smells like gardenias. Or orchids."

"Orchids don't smell," Lizzie says crossly.

Belle glares at her. "Violets, then. She loved fancy soap, she used to rub it on her wrists before we went to the Artists' Union dances. Nobody could afford perfume back then."

"All right. What's next?"

"New sheets," Belle says. "Get some flowered ones. A reading lamp for her night table. And books. Hardbacks. You choose them for her, she's literary, like you. Get her some poetry. Her husband was a poet." A car slows down on the bend outside the house; Lizzie freezes. "What poets do you like?" Belle asks loudly.

Lizzie tries to remember; it's like reaching back through a fog. "Wordsworth," she says, though she's not sure she does anymore. "Wallace Stevens. Sir Thomas Wyatt. Wouldn't you like to go to bed now?"

"No, I wouldn't. As a matter of fact. Get the cards."

And so they play endless games of gin, the grotesque faces of the jacks and the queens flung down on the scuffed oak of the table, while the clock ticks, the refrigerator hums, one car after another slows on the curve and picks up speed again. Every time it happens, Belle fixes Lizzie with a grim, bullying stare, as though forbidding her even to try to tell if it's Sam's truck out there. Lizzie turns defiantly towards the window, trying anyway, but the truth is, she cannot really concentrate; while Belle is looking at her that way, she cannot even yearn wholeheartedly for Paul's return. And strangely, once the car passes, she feels a sudden calmness descend, a flash of blessed clarity, as though the vast mindless creature that had her in its grip has given her back to herself for a moment.

Finally, after two cars have gone by in rapid succession, Belle lays down her cards and leans back. "All right, that's enough. I'm going to bed now." Lizzie wonders if the effort of fending off all that longing has been too much for her. Feeling contrite, she helps Belle rise from her chair and escorts her down the hall.

"There's no need for you to stay," Belle says gruffly at the dining room door.

"I know." She has always left the room or turned her back when Nina was undressing Belle; now she watches in silence as Belle lowers herself onto the bed and forces first one shoe and then the other — gray loafer-like wedgies, made of squishy plastic — off with the opposite foot. Then she reaches behind her back, with a little grunt, and starts pulling at her baggy blue shift.

"Here," Lizzie says, approaching the bed. She tugs awkwardly at the front of the dress, until Belle, in sudden surrender, lifts her arms over her head and lets Lizzie get on with it.

She has a moment of panic at Belle's nakedness, the sad white skin splotched with purple veins, the elastic of bra and pants cutting into rolls of sagging flesh; averting her eyes, she fishes under the pillow for the green cotton nightgown Nina ironed that morning. When she turns around, Belle has removed the bra and is hunched forward, in nothing but her frayed nylon pants, staring at the floor. "Here," Lizzie says again, in a thickened voice, and Belle looks up at her with such a mixture of shame and defiance that she can hardly bear it. Quickly, she holds out the nightgown, an offer of dignity restored. Belle's arms come up once more, and Lizzie draws the thin cotton over her head, pulling it past her wrinkled breasts. Belle raises her head, mercifully herself again.

"Get me a glass of water, please."

By the time Lizzie returns, she has managed to swing her legs onto the bed; it only remains to pull up the top sheet and the worn blanket. This Lizzie does, a little nervously. Belle is watching her with a beady eye; some special sarcasm may be forthcoming, to restore the balance of power.

But instead she merely says, "Good night," switching off the bedside lamp. Lizzie is half-way to the door when she speaks again. "I used to scrub the floors."

"What?"

"When he stayed out. It was a way of passing the time."

Lizzie imagines her on her hands and knees, listening to the water sloshing over the wide wooden boards in the silence she never got used to; she imagines the darkness outside the windows, the faint light from the wood stove, the kerosene lamp sitting on the kitchen table.

"The joke is, time would have passed no matter what I did," Belle says, and then, while Lizzie stands there waiting, she falls asleep, her breath transformed into a series of low growls. For a minute Lizzie stays there, strangely comforted by the sound; when she finally closes the door behind her she is breathing in the same uneven rhythm, her chest rising and falling in time with Belle's snores.

22

THE NEXT THING LIZZIE KNOWS, SHE WAKES IN A cold kitchen, with the radio buzzing beside her like a fly in a bottle. Outside, the sky has gone from pinkish-blue to a faded navy, streaked with opalescent cloud. Stumbling to the window, she sees, beyond the trees, a more concentrated light blazing through the dark. The very thought that Paul is there, eighty yards away, that she can see him just by crossing the lawn to the studio, makes the whole shaky barrier that Belle erected totter and fall. A minute later, she is hurrying across the damp grass, not noticing the stars or the moon or the sound of the wind overhead.

She is startled at how chilly the studio feels at night, with the heating off and the harsh white glare of the track lights overhead. And there he sits, in the khaki workshirt she sometimes wears in his loft at night, propped against the wall in the far corner. He nods briefly at her and leans his head back again.

"What are you doing?" she asks stupidly, stopping halfway across the floor.

"What am I doing." His voice is slow, gloomy, with a trace of irritation; he doesn't seem in any way pleased to see her. "It's what I'm not doing that's the real point."

"What do you mean?"

He looks at her gravely for a moment before shutting his eyes. "I mean the things that count are the things you suddenly find you can't do."

"Has Sam been giving you coke?"

"Sam . . . Jesus. Sam," he says, back to his normal self for a moment. "Poor guy. He wants power so bad it's driving him nuts." He turns solemn again. "It's got nothing to do with Sam. He can't touch this one."

"What one? What are you trying to say?"

"It's what we can't do . . . that's how we'll be judged in the end. Do you understand that?"

"I don't know what you're talking about." Her resentment comes flooding back: he has forgotten about the sunset, about the promise he made; he has not given her a thought tonight.

He sighs heavily. "I didn't come in here just to see where he painted those paintings, okay? I came in here to find something."

"What?"

"Never mind what. Just something someone wanted me to find. But I couldn't do it, you know why?"

"No."

He looks at her accusingly. "You don't seem to realize, Lizzie, this is important, I'm trying to tell you about something that matters to me. Something about my immortal soul."

"Then go ahead and tell me."

He leans back again, aggrieved. "I couldn't do it because I remembered him . . . Madden. I started imagining what it was like when he was working in here, before the fancy lighting was installed, or the radiators, when it was still just your basic old shed, with the wind coming through the cracks. And he came out here one night and just to keep warm he started dancing. With a can of paint and a stick and a big brush he'd been painting the house with. I remembered how I used to see him in my mind, dancing that dance of his" — his eyes are bright with tears — "and, oh shit, Lizzie. What the fuck happened? It used to be you did art because you loved it, and then your family disowned you and everyone knew you were going to starve in a garret, but it was the only thing you could imagine doing with your life. And now we're all dirty, me as much as anyone." The tears are flowing down his cheeks now, into his beard. "There's no innocence left. I don't even know if I love it anymore." But she cannot help thinking that he is crying for himself, he is not crying for her, or even for Clay Madden. She makes a little, involuntary sound, a click of annoyance, and he looks at her indignantly.

"You don't understand what I'm talking about, do you?"

She digs her nails into her palms. "I do understand. I do. But we were going to go to the beach and watch the sun set."

"Oh, Christ. I grew up on a beach, I've seen enough sunsets to last me a lifetime. I'm talking about art here. And honor. I thought you'd have some faint inkling of what those things mean."

"Stop that. Stop sneering at me. All I'm saying is, it's always your art, it's always your honor."

"Okay, Lizzie." Slowly, he gets to his feet. "Let's talk about you instead. Let's talk about your art, and your honor. All right? You start. Go ahead."

"You don't think I have anything to say. Because I don't know about art, I don't know about honor, that's what you mean."

"Oh, shit. You're twenty-five years old, for God's sake. You're still a baby."

"Then what are you doing with me?"

"What?"

"Why are you hanging out with someone who's too young to have honor?"

He clears his throat nervously. "Listen, Lizzie, I've got other things on my mind. Go back to the house, why don't you, and I'll be over in a little while."

"What other things? What were you looking for?"

"I don't want to discuss it."

"Is that why you came out this weekend? To find this thing, whatever it was?"

"Don't be ridiculous."

"I know you didn't come just to visit me. But I thought it was about him, and meeting Miss Prokoff. Is there something else?"

"I told you, I didn't do anything."

"Because of your honor. Not for my sake, or because she was nice to you. For the sake of your honor."

"You're really ticking me off now."

"I suppose honor doesn't have to do with actual people. It's all abstract, like painting."

"This isn't funny anymore. I'm going back to the house, you can turn off the lights when you leave. And shut the door behind you."

As he is heading out, she says, "You were looking for Maddens, weren't you?"

He turns around.

"Nina told me how people always think there are Maddens hidden here, but there aren't. So you don't have to worry about your honor. There's nothing to find."

"As a matter of fact, there is," he says.

They stare at each other.

"I thought you didn't look."

"I did look, I just didn't take anything. And I'm not going to tell anyone, either. That's what I meant when I said I couldn't do it. But if you go to that drawing cabinet over there and check out the bottom drawer, there's a whole batch of oils on paper. Eleven of them. She's been really clever, she hid them underneath some of her drawings, way at the back, in the very last drawer you look in. By that time you don't really think you're going to find anything. But they're there. The question is, why the hell does she keep them out here?"

"Because she likes to look at them sometimes."

"Did she tell you that?"

"No. I just know."

"She didn't mention them to you, did she?"

"No. But who were you going to tell if you did tell someone?"

He looks away from her. "Just someone I met."

"But who? Tell me."

"Someone who wanted to show the stuff. Okay?"

A thought strikes her. "Was it that dealer you went to see the other day?"

Now he starts to laugh. He shakes his head, chortling, as though she has done something adorable.

"What's so funny?"

"Nothing. I just forget sometimes how smart you are."

"So it *was* that woman."

"Yeah, it was. Now lay off, would you?"

"I thought she liked your work."

"Sure she does," he says, grinding his teeth. "She loves my work. So much that if I find out about Prokoff's early Maddens, if I give ol' Sasha a list with dates and sizes, maybe even slip out a few things for her to look at, she'll put me in a show. Now do you get it? Do you see how fucking ugly the whole thing is?"

"I'm sorry," Lizzie says, and means it; for the first time, in a way she hardly grasps, he has become not her fantasy of him but simply himself, older than she ever acknowledges, with furrows in his forehead and leathery skin on his neck.

He wipes his nose on his arm, streaking his face with dirt. "I think I'm going to get out of New York. Out in the country, like Colorado or some place like that. And just paint my brains out till I die."

"What about us?" she asks. "What's going to happen to us?"

He looks at her sadly. "Come on, Lizzie, there is no us, you know that. There can't be an us."

"I love you," she says, though she knows he doesn't want her to. She's always known she isn't supposed to say it, which is why it comes out sounding not like a declaration but a plea for forgiveness.

"Don't," he says, stricken. "You make me feel like such a shit." He pats her clumsily on the shoulder, like a Victorian uncle. "You'll get over it. Wait and see. In a year you'll be glad you're rid of me."

"I just want you to be happy, that's all. And you're not going to be happy in Colorado, I know that. I want you to stay in New York." She is sobbing as a child might, for a treat she's been denied. Even to herself what she is saying makes no sense, but she hardly cares. Suddenly she is so tired she can barely stand.

"Go to bed, Lizzie, okay? Go on now. I'll be along in a minute." He puts a hand under her arm, to steer her. "Be a good girl. We'll talk about it in the morning." But she shakes her head and ducks away.

"I don't want to go to bed. I want to stay here with you." Already panic is setting in: how will she bear the silence when she's alone, how can she ever have children if they are not his? She still half-hopes that it will turn out right — he will say he didn't mean it, about there not being an us; he is just stoned, drunk, tired; of course he loves her, of course they are going to be together forever.

But he, not being a great reader of novels, fails to play the scene correctly; he only stands there embarrassed, waiting for her to go.

Outside, the wind is rising. It is a night full of unsettled noises, half swallowed by the rushing dark. Doors bang, the surf moans, branches rustle and creak, but over and above that floats an edgy feeling, the sense that at any moment something calamitous may happen. Twenty-eight years ago on this date, a black Buick hurtled around a bend just half a mile from where they are standing. While Clay Madden howled with laughter, it skidded on the gravel and crashed into a tree at ninety miles an hour.

23

THE NEXT MORNING, AS LIZZIE LIES GRIEVING OVER-
head, Belle drags herself painfully to the bathroom, clinging to
Sam's rails for support. She has forgotten about Lizzie's problems;
she is thinking, with a quickening in her blood, of Mark Dudley's
impending visit and the terrible things he will force her to say.
Everyone has been placating her for so long that it's been years
since she's had a chance to do battle. She realizes that she is looking forward to it.

Lizzie hears Belle's footsteps in the hallway and gets out of
bed, imagining that rescue is at hand. All night she has been frightened by the thought that maybe she does not exist, that maybe if
she turned on the light and looked in the mirror, no one would be
there. She stumbles downstairs in her pajamas and waits anxiously for Belle to emerge from the bathroom and reassure her.

But Belle has been enjoying her imaginary tête-à-tête with
Mark Dudley, acting out both their roles and trouncing him every
time. She is not in the mood to play nursemaid.

"What are you doing up at this hour? Go back to bed."

Lizzie bursts into tears, covering her face with her hands, while
Belle struggles to contain her annoyance.

"I gather you didn't make it up with your young man."

Lizzie shakes her head mutely.

"In that case, the best thing to do is to get some sleep."

"I can't sleep. I tried, but I can't."

A sharp, exasperated sound escapes from Belle's throat. "Then make us a cup of tea."

It is not much of a reprieve, but Lizzie takes it, heading for the kitchen with tears stinging her eyes. What torments her at the moment is the thought that maybe she failed him in sympathy; she thought only of herself. This is not something, however, that she can discuss with Belle, who has followed her into the kitchen and seated herself, with a grimace, at the oak table. Lizzie sets her mug of chamomile before her.

"Do you think I can phone Sam yet?"

"I think they get up early," Lizzie says, wondering how long she can feel this bad without dying.

"I need to find out if that man is coming."

"What man?"

"Mark Dudley," Belle says irritably. "The biographer. What's the date today?"

"The sixteenth."

"That's what I thought. This afternoon I want you to drive me to the bay." But Lizzie is silent, no longer able to keep up her part in this dialogue. "What's gotten into you?" Belle asks, having forgotten again.

"It's over," Lizzie wails. It's not that she still hopes for comfort, more that she cannot stop herself; the hunger to release her misery is too great. "It's completely over."

"Here. Have a Kleenex." Belle waits until Lizzie has finished blowing her nose before saying sternly, "It's nonsense to say it's over after one fight."

"It's not like that . . . it's never been right. He just doesn't care that much. He doesn't need me."

"Thank God," Belle says fiercely. "You should count yourself lucky. Now bring your list from last night. There are things I want to add."

Mostly, however, she repeats herself: there is the soap, there are the flowers from the garden, there is the poetry — "No modern poets. She'll brood about her husband, his books didn't sell." A van must be rented, with room for a wheelchair; a reading lamp must be bought. Sam's help must be enlisted, to get her in and out of the chair. "What time is it?"

"Seven thirty-five."

"I'll call him at eight fifteen." She looks out the window, at a fat orange bird pulling up a worm on the lawn. "Do you know what a *yortsayt* is?"

Lizzie shakes her head.

"It's the anniversary of a death. Twenty-eight years ago today my husband died."

"I'm sorry."

"When you're old you won't remember why you were crying this morning. You won't be nostalgic for your younger self, or your lost loves, or any of it. That won't matter any more. What will haunt you is everything you didn't do when you should have. You never get over that."

" 'We have left undone those things which we ought to have done; And we have done those things which we ought not to have done; And there is no health in us.' "

"Who said that?"

"It's from the *Book of Common Prayer*," Lizzie says, and then, when Belle looks blank, "The Episcopal prayer book. The old version."

"Say it again."

Lizzie does.

"So the Christians knew all along."

"But what can I do?" Lizzie says. "I mean, right now?"

"You can help me get dressed, for a start. I have to look presentable when that man shows up."

By ten o'clock, they are all assembled: Belle resplendent in a reddish-brown tent dress slightly less shabby than her others; Sam to lay the cable on the stairs, Nina to make a stew from the lamb she thinks needs using up; Paul to assist Sam, who laughed when he heard Paul wasn't up yet and went to wake him. "We did a few bars last night," he said. Paul was particularly friendly to Belle, talking to her with great animation about the Caravaggio show at the Met. But he never looked at Lizzie.

At 11:30, Sam announces that he is finished; the larch and cherrywood chair he has made can be installed the next morning. "You want to take a quick run over to the point?" he asks Paul, and then turns to Lizzie. "Is he allowed out today?"

"He can go anywhere he likes," she says stonily.

"I'll bring him back in plenty of time for lunch."

But already she has turned away, heading up the stairs for the bathroom, where she stares at her face in the mirror for a long minute. It is all there at least, definitely a person: eyes, nose, lips, wavy hair the color of vanilla toffee. She can just detect faint traces of lines around her mouth, like news from the future: they are telling her that she has a life span; she has been given a certain allotment of years, and some of them are gone. Then she hears Sam's truck rattling out of the drive, and leans against the mirror, shutting her eyes.

At 11:48, as she is washing her face, the front doorbell rings. Footsteps, presumably Nina's, cross the hall; a man's voice is just audible; Belle's stick strikes on wood. Then the pocket doors to the living room, which are always kept open, rumble shut. Lizzie sneaks downstairs and out the kitchen door, to walk to the beach she never reached with Paul. The sky is a luminous blue, translucent with sun; a red Jaguar with leather seats is parked in Belle's drive, its chrome trim glinting. For the first time, it occurs to Lizzie that people might find comfort even in sportscars.

Ten minutes later, as the road curves and the bay opens out before her — the shouts of children reach her from the shore — fat drops of rain spatter onto her hair. Soon, though the sun is still hot, a freak summer shower soaks the top of her head and sends her scuttling for the imperfect shelter of a stunted pine. Then the picnickers from the beach start hurrying towards her, clutching their books and children and blankets; she too heads back, meaning to dart upstairs and hide in her room. But when she arrives at the house, Sam's truck is back in the drive, behind the Jaguar, and voices are coming through an open window.

First an English one: "Can't you see that Miss Prokoff and I are having a serious discussion?"

Then Paul's: "Come on, let's go."

Now Belle's: "Don't leave on my account. As far as I'm concerned, the discussion is over."

The Englishman again: "I refuse to believe you mean that."

"Anyway, they have as much right to be here as you do," Belle says. "You can't order people out of my house."

"You there, you look like a sensible chap. Why don't you take your friend and leave us?"

Paul again: "Knock it off, would you. A sensible chap. You condescending pommy bastard."

"I don't believe this. This is simply preposterous."

Sam: "Hey, you heard the lady. We got as much right to be here as you do. You pommy bastard." He laughs, a high cackling laugh. "What the hell's that mean, anyway?"

"It's a term of disapprobation the Ozzies have for we English."

"Us English," Paul says. "Even I know that. Shit. You're a right old fraud, aren't you? You probably grew up in a council flat somewhere, you picked up that posh accent from the telly. But I bet the Yanks eat it up."

Lizzie can't bear to miss this; on a surge of adrenaline, she rushes inside and heads for the living room, where Mark Dudley seems frozen in the act of rising from his chair. Three feet away stands Sam, streaked with dirt but looking more than ever like Jesus, his blue eyes blazing in his thin face. Paul, too, stationed at Sam's side, is dirty and disheveled, a rip in the knee of his jeans, the ordinary stains of cadmium and cobalt and burnt ocher under his nails obscured by smears of loamy dirt.

Belle, on the velvet couch, is the only one to acknowledge

Lizzie's presence. "Come in," she says, with a magisterial nod, and turns back to Mark Dudley. "You still haven't told me what you copied from my journals."

"Go ahead," Sam says, glowering at Dudley. "Answer the question."

"I didn't copy anything."

"I don't believe you."

"It's the truth. The old cow wouldn't let me."

"She's my dearest friend."

"Apologize," Sam says.

"I am not going to apologize. She hasn't spoken to the woman in forty years."

"I saw her yesterday," Belle tells him. "She didn't care for you much, either."

"She certainly acted as though she did. She wanted me to come and read Shakespeare to her. The love poems."

"Would you like me to hit him?" Sam asks.

"No, thank you." She turns back to Dudley. "Who else have you talked to?"

"I'm not going to answer that."

"Why not?"

"I have to protect my sources."

"You mean they've said such awful things about me you don't dare tell me their names."

"Perhaps I can write about this little scene. I may even start the book with it: the widow's thugs threatening the biographer on a summer afternoon. That ought to sell a few copies."

"All right, scumbag," Sam says.

"Fuckwit." This from Paul.

"Say you're sorry to the lady."

"For what?"

"For existing," Paul says. "For feeding off artists' flesh."

"Stop that," Belle says, and then, to Mark Dudley, "Listen to me. I'll give you the names of people to talk to, all right? I'll tell them to cooperate. I'll even authorize it if you insist. All I ask is to look over what you've written before it's published. That's fairly common practice, isn't it?"

"I'm not interested in writing that sort of book."

"What sort of book?"

"The sort you'd authorize." He looks at her with genuine curiosity. "Why do you care so much, anyway?"

"I don't need to be gossiped about at my age. All those old rumors were finally getting buried, and you want to dig them up again."

"I'm not planning to dig up old rumors. I'm planning to tell the truth."

"People remember things wrong, you know. Especially things that happened forty years ago. They get mixed up between something they saw themselves and something they read afterwards. I do it myself. And that's when they're not even trying to make trouble. How will you know whose truth is truer than the next person's?"

"I have a good ear, Mrs. Madden. A good nose. And I generally manage to get to the bottom of things, one way or another."

"Then publish it after I'm dead."

"You can't force me to do that."

She shuts her eyes. "I'm not forcing you, Mr. Dudley. I'm asking you. I'm entreating you. All right?"

"I'm sorry."

"Don't you care about being decent?"

"It wouldn't be decent at all. I'd be waiting around for you to die."

"That wouldn't bother me," Belle says, with a short laugh. "Believe me."

"Well, it would bother me." He leans towards her, his voice suddenly intimate. "Tell me something."

"What?"

"What did you do with the painting he promised that girl?"

"He never promised her any painting," she says shrilly.

"It was purple, she said. With a lot of gray in it, and traces of orange. I haven't been able to find any record of it. Not even in the catalogue raisonée."

"That's because it never existed."

"Didn't it?"

"What are you suggesting? Are you saying I got rid of it?"

"I'm just asking."

"You think I'd destroy one of his paintings? You don't understand anything."

"So explain it to me."

"She's lying to you. About the painting, about everything. She was the one that made him get in the car that night. He'd been invited to a party, you see, at a big fancy house by the pond. He didn't want to go, but she did. She had her black dress on, and her cultured pearls, she wanted to preen herself in front of his rich friends. She got bored staying home with a drunk."

"You can't know that for sure. You weren't there."

"The man who gave the party told me what happened. He phoned to say he wasn't coming, and the girl was whining in the background."

"Are you saying the accident was her fault? You can't really believe that."

"I'm telling you what really went on that night. Which is more than she'll ever do."

"I think you knew when you left he wouldn't be there when you got back. Maybe that was what you wanted. If you couldn't have him no one could. So you went away that summer to let it happen. Because he wanted to die, didn't he? Bad enough so he didn't care if he took her with him. He wasn't any sort of hero then, just another lush who'd made a mess of things. One more drunken bastard in a souped-up car."

"All right, scumbag," Sam says, and lunges at Dudley, his right fist shooting towards his head. Dudley leans sideways just in time, so the punch only grazes his temple. Paul grabs Sam from behind and starts dragging him towards the door, but Sam shakes him off and heads for Dudley again, both fists raised.

Meanwhile Belle is rising to her feet, or trying to. "Stop that," she cries, and then totters, stumbles, leans back to steady herself, and loses her balance. One leg shoots out from under her; she crashes onto the floor, face first, with a horrifying thud.

"Oh my God," Lizzie screams, rushing to her, while the three men stand frozen. She kneels down to lift Belle's head, to gather her in her arms, and then remembers she mustn't. "Are you all right?" she asks instead, stupidly. "Can you hear me?" Belle does not answer, but it is clear, at least, that she is breathing; a hoarse whistling sound emerges from her throat.

Nina appears in the doorway, and the three men start moving towards Belle. "Don't move her," Lizzie says accusingly, getting to her feet. She goes to the telephone and dials 911. "Yes," she says, having given the address, "she had a fall" — looking at Sam — "yes, she's unconscious. I don't know, I don't know about her spine. I only know she's alive."

"Now look what you've done," Dudley says, but half-heartedly, without conviction. Nina marches over to Sam. "You've got to go," she says, taking hold of his arm. "You've got to get out of here." She turns to Lizzie, her face ashen. "Don't you see, if they know he was here, they'll think it was his fault somehow."

"It was his fault."

"It was all their faults."

"You're a good woman," says Paul hoarsely, which Lizzie takes as a reproach to herself.

Silently, she returns to Belle's side and sits on the floor beside her, touching, very tentatively, the stiff gray hairs on the back of her head. She cannot see Belle's face, but she knows, somehow, that this is the right thing to do. She strokes Belle's hair; her scalp seems much too fragile, the veins just under the skin. She strokes her arm, her hand, her shoulder, touches her head again. "It's all right," she says, "you're going to be all right." She prays that it's true, though she is horribly afraid that she is lying.

24

BY THE TIME THE MEDICS ARRIVE, WITH THEIR FOLD-UP
stretcher and complex networks of straps, they are confronted by a
roomful of women. Sam has hurried away; Mark Dudley, having
pressed Lizzie's hand and promised to stay in touch, has roared off
in his Jaguar. Paul has vanished upstairs, claiming an urgent need
to wash his hands.

Nina remains, but her old, serene authority is gone; she hovers
uncertainly, waiting for Lizzie to tell her what to do, while Lizzie
goes on whispering reassurances to Belle. Finally Nina kneels on
Belle's other side, to take her hand and murmur her own words of
comfort, but with one eye on Lizzie, who cannot meet her gaze. "O
Lord, look down from heaven, behold, visit and relieve this thy servant," Lizzie says under her breath, in case there's a God after all.
Then she remembers that Jesus will be invoked soon, and stops in
confusion: Belle is presumably denied the consolation of Jesus.
Meanwhile, Belle's breathing continues, a harsh rasping sound that
does not encourage optimism.

A minute later, the two medics enter side by side, stolid and
grave, like professional mourners. "Step back a minute, please," the
older one says, in a deep bass voice, and crouches on the floor, feeling Belle's pulse. The other raises Belle's head — Lizzie has a glimpse
of skin as gray as wood ash — so the other can shine a flashlight at
her eyes. "Reactive, uhhuh, accommodating, uhhuh." They cover

her with a spongy blanket the color of pink lemonade, and prepare the stretcher to receive her.

"Is she going to be all right?" Lizzie asks.

The one who wielded the flashlight looks at her sternly. "We really can't tell you that."

"But do you know?"

Ignoring this question, the medic sets to work arranging the straps, while his associate looks around the room as though to memorize it. "I never thought I'd get inside this house," he says to no one in particular.

"There'll probably be an inquiry about the accident," the other man says, straightening up from his task. "You'll have to give statements."

"Fine," Lizzie says, "we'll do that," and then, because Belle's breathing seems harsher than ever, "I wish you'd take her to the hospital now." Belle's skin has turned a waxy ivory, with blue undertones; her eyes seem to have sunk much deeper into their sockets since this morning. But the men never look at her face as they transfer her to the stretcher; all their attention is on the procedure itself, the lifting and strapping and punching of numbers into a tiny pager.

"Can we come with her?" Lizzie asks. The older one explains, more Olympian than ever, that only the next of kin are allowed in the ambulance; she and Nina will have to get to the hospital on their own.

Nina, however, hardly seems to be thinking about Belle. "What will you say in your statement?" she cries, as soon as the men have carried Belle out.

Lizzie tries not to sound reproachful. "Don't worry about it," she says stiffly. "Sam didn't do anything on purpose, I'll tell them that."

"They won't believe it. They hate him, the police out here, they've really got it in for him."

"I can't help that," Lizzie says, "I can't lie to them. Please don't ask me to do that."

Nina puts a hand on her arm. "Of course you can't . . . I'm just

worried, that's all. Especially because . . . how things are right now."
Lizzie looks at her blankly. "I'm pregnant," Nina says, a thrill of
pride in her voice. "I wanted to tell her since Wednesday, I was just
waiting for the right time."

All Lizzie can think is that Nina will never leave Sam now. And
then, ashamed, she gives Nina an awkward hug. Nina beams, her
face more radiant than ever.

"When is it due?"

"Mid-March, the doctor says. I thought if it was a girl maybe
I'd name it after her." Her smile fades. "I'm just scared they'll make
trouble for Sam."

"Sam will be all right," Lizzie says, with more conviction than
she feels. She bites her lip. "You shouldn't worry, it's bad for the
baby."

"Oh, I know. I just can't help it. Where are you going?"

"I'll be back in a minute," Lizzie says, edging towards the
stairs. Because of course she too has been thinking of someone else.

She expects him to be in the bathroom, cleaning up, but
instead he has entered Belle's bedroom to stare at the high dark bed
with the carved pineapples where Lizzie has slept for the past two
nights. She watches him in silence for a minute, noticing for the
first time the uneven curve of his hairline, where it is receding.
Finally she coughs, and he looks around.

"Did they take her to the hospital?"

"Yes."

"So you'll be going too."

"In a minute. What are you doing in here?"

"I might never be in this house again. I wanted to see where he
slept."

"She could die," Lizzie says fiercely. "Can't you think about
her for a change?"

He shrugs. "She probably won't die, she's pretty tough."

"But what if she does?"

"She'll still have had a lot more years than he ever got."

"You really don't care. You think because she's not a genius she's got no right to be alive anyway."

"Stop it," he says, but kindly, without rancor. "That's not why you're mad at me. You're mad because of last night."

The fact that this is true only makes her madder.

"Nina is pregnant," she says, hurling the words like an accusation: surely that should make him see, though what it is he's supposed to see she's not quite sure.

"I suppose that's my fault too."

"I didn't say it was your fault."

"Then why are you telling me? What's it got to do with anything?"

She never knew he looked like this, this ungainly amalgam of bones, angles, flesh. Her heart is not heavy but achingly light, swelling minute by minute into her chest.

"What is it?" he asks, when she continues to stand there.

"Nothing. There's food downstairs if you want it."

"Thanks."

"That's okay." She realizes she is lingering not out of wistfulness, not because she really hopes for much anymore, but because as long as she is bickering with him she can fend off the fear. When she goes downstairs, Belle will not be there; the ride to the hospital is in front of her, and then a vigil in a room at the end of a hallway, with the tubes and the monitors and memories of her mother. Right now she would give ten years of her life, she would trade all of Paul's paintings and Clay Madden's too, to be sitting in the kitchen with Belle as she was that morning.

Not this again, Belle thinks, not this crap again, as she is wheeled down a hallway on a cold metal trolley, like a slab of meat, with colors heaving behind her eyes. And then they navigate a corner, the motion ceases, a curtain is yanked shut. She opens her eyes to see someone loitering in the gap of the fabric, a man with a cup in his hand; the smell of coffee floats through the air, making her gag, and she falls for a long time into blackness.

Ernest was standing in the kitchen doorway, frowning at her.

"Do you want some coffee?"

"No, I do not want coffee. Or soup. Or home-made bread. What exactly do you suppose you're doing?"

"What are you talking about?"

"Do you think you're keeping him alive, is that it?"

"Is that what?"

"Why you don't do the sensible thing and get out. It's a form of arrogance, you realize that. If he's going to die he'll die anyway. You can't prevent it."

"What makes you so sure?"

"If you really believe that, you must believe yourself possessed of magic powers. And if your will can operate so potently when you're here, why not when you're elsewhere? Why can't you exercise this feat of mind control from a distance?"

"I'd like some coffee, even if you wouldn't."

"He's out there in that car, which you should have taken away from him months ago. He could be dead at this very moment."

"No, he isn't."

"How do you know that?"

"I just do."

"You've got to get out. Andrea Poole from MOMA is leaving for France on the eighteenth. You could go with her."

"I don't have the money."

"I'll lend it to you, damn it."

"I owe too much money already. Besides, I don't want to travel with Andrea, she talks all the time."

"In that case, go with someone else. Go alone. Do something. Are you staying just to prove how tough you are?"

"I don't need your wisdom right now."

"Then what do you need?"

She was almost sorry for him. He really thought she could tell him; he imagined there was something she might ask for, some missing element that, once supplied, could solve her problem. He believed that reason, judiciously applied, would triumph, just as the feed-and-grain salesman's widow down the road believed in the efficacy of prayer and pressed little pamphlets on her, well-thumbed, with verses from the *New Testament*. Everyone, it seemed, had faith in something; everyone knew of a Jungian analyst, a vitamin-rich diet, a regimen of cold baths and apomorphine that had worked wonders for somebody just like Clay. The night before she had caught him talking to the girl on the phone. "What are you wearing now, honey?" he was asking with a snigger, and when Belle walked in, he winked at her and kept on talking. Meanwhile the tears spilled down his face as fast as ever. Let Ernest apply reason to that.

"I told you, I want some coffee," she said, and stood up.

He made an exasperated sound. "'Too long a sacrifice'" — rocking back and forth on his heels — "'Too long a sacrifice can make a stone of the heart.' I finally see what he meant."

"Are you leaving already?"

"There seems no point in remaining here. But remember what I said. Think it over."

Three weeks later, Clay brought the girl to the house, and she called the police and had her removed from the property. The next day, she borrowed the money and booked her passage. In the dreams she had on the voyage, the ship pitched and heaved and plunged into icy water, a train careened off the track, her house burst into flames while she stood on the lawn, watching. But she'd been dreaming those things all summer; she no longer believed they were portents of anything real.

It is not that she can't see, or doesn't understand, where she is; she knows this is Lizzie, gripping the rail by the bed, with Nina beside her, her eyes round and sorrowful. The metal of the trolley is cold against her back, penetrating the thin pad they have placed beneath her. She can dimly make out a machine, an awkward crane-like contraption with a bag dangling from its top, and a blinking screen. But she is back in the room in Paris, with a stuffed golden bird in a painted birdcage, two spindly brocaded chairs, double doors leading to a balcony. She and Andrea are eating an elegant French breakfast — strong coffee, sweet butter, croissants, plum jam — when the phone rings. She seems to have known forever, only she has forgotten, and then it is there, an infinity of never, the void made flesh. The past has been severed from the future, nobody can ever join them again.

Someone in the room starts sobbing, Lizzie probably, which irritates her, when there is so much to do: soap to buy, for one thing, lemon verbena — that's the kind she meant. The chairlift must be finished, the table must be moved into the garden, the shiny new books stacked beside Sophie's bed. She is not going to die, not now, before Sophie arrives. She has got to show up on Wednesday with that rented van, or Sophie will think she has betrayed her again.

Rallying herself to speak, she supposes that the pressure in her skull is caused by the words gathering momentum there; she imagines that her will has generated the rush of heat to her head. She opens her mouth, and her face convulses, a gurgle emerges from her throat. Fluid is surging into the crevices of her brain. While they stare at her in terror, while the doctor, on his way to her bedside, stops in the corridor for a minute, to talk to one of the nurses, her soul, the hard kernel of consciousness that is Belle Prokoff, shuts, opens, shuts again. She sees and fails to see; light breaks in and vanishes; she watches it recede, registers its return. Then she goes blind forever.

25

IN HER TAPESTRIED BEDROOM IN THE WINE COUNTRY, Rosie Dreyfus dreams that she and Belle are riding together in an elevator in the Seagram Building. She is explaining to Belle, who listens meekly, that she doesn't care about modern art any more, she hasn't kept a single painting from that time. "That was your big mistake," she tells her, "you could never let go of the past. You would have been a lot happier if you'd learned how to forget." In the dream, she feels a surge of triumph as she says this, but when she wakes up she discovers that she is crying.

In the nursing home in Ardsley, the phone rings fourteen times in the room that Sophie Aronow, née Horowitz, shares with an Italian grandmother and a retired postmistress from the Bronx. Sophie is out on the porch, listening to a tape of Wallace Stevens that her niece has sent her. But Lizzie, trying again an hour later, catches her as she is wheeled back to her room to fetch a sweater and breaks the news. "I'm so sorry," Lizzie says, her voice catching. Sophie gestures to the attendant to leave her.

"You didn't kill her, did you?"

"Of course not."

"Then why are you apologizing?"

"You sound just like her," Lizzie says, starting to cry.

"Stop that. Was it an accident? A stroke? Tell me."

Hiccuping, Lizzie tells her about the scene in the living room — about Sam (but not Paul), and Mark Dudley saying that Clay

Madden was just a drunk and Belle wanted him dead. "She got mad at him because he said she wouldn't give some woman a painting. And then Sam threw a punch, and she tried to stand up, and she toppled over."

"I can't listen to this," Sophie says. "I'm hanging up now. Where can I reach you later?"

"I'm still at her house. I have to give a statement about the accident."

"So you'll call me in an hour. Please."

Cast adrift, Lizzie roams the house, staring at all the objects that have survived their owner. Belle's cane lies at a crooked angle in front of the living room couch, the blue blanket is neatly folded at the foot of the hospital bed, the dark blue bowl still sits on the hall table. And upstairs, on the landing, Belle's face looks out at her brazenly from the self-portrait, with the same scowl of defiance as before, the same aggressive thrust of the chin.

Anyone can see she was going to suffer, that girl; anyone can see it was no accident, what happened to her. She brought it on herself. She was courting disaster, flaunting herself heedlessly before fate, with her recklessness, her truculence, her unreasonable demands on life; she should have known it would exact retribution in the end.

But maybe it wasn't like that at all. Maybe it was just a fluke, her suffering, not destiny but random chance; maybe nothing she'd done or failed to do had brought about her downfall. That would be infinitely worse, that would mean there were no safeguards against calamity. In which case, how can Lizzie prepare, how can she protect herself against whatever bad luck might be lying in wait, like the car that leapt onto the pavement to destroy her mother? She's afraid that nothing she does, no amount of virtue or hard work or planning, can guarantee her a happy ending.

In the study of his apartment on Claremont Avenue, Ernest sits in the semi-darkness, gripping the arms of his chair. So many people he's known have died in the last few years that death should not come as a surprise any longer. An Augustan melancholy is what's called for, some lofty reflections on mortality. He has always been an expert at those. But not this churning in his stomach, not this fear and desolation, like an abandoned child.

He is remembering things he hasn't thought of in years. The afternoon she told him, in her nasal Brooklyn voice, in the middle of a crowded gallery, that Clay Madden was a great painter. The morning she came chasing after him on Eighth Street, when he was just about to board a bus, to tell him breathlessly but without any trace of embarrassment that Clay was in jail again, could he come with her to the lockup to get him out? When he went to look at the paintings Madden wanted in his first show, she stayed in the room the whole time, her arms folded belligerently across her chest, prepared to step in and tell him off if he didn't praise them enough. The afternoon that he went to the house and told her to leave her husband, she insisted on making coffee.

And then all those years she was alone, like him, she kept him married to the world; they meddled freely in each other's lives, phoning each other nearly every day to continue their argument. She never asked of him anything he could not give. Now he feels as though he's surrounded by too much space, as though his voice, if he spoke, would send back an echo.

But he must take care of business. The place in Manhattan, with its doorman and its alarm system, doesn't worry him; the Long Island house, though, is vulnerable to all kinds of intruders: curiosity-seekers, local teenagers wanting a place to party, journalists looking for a scoop. For all he knows, there could even be Maddens hidden right on the premises: it would have been just like her to keep one under the bed. So he calls the house to see if anyone is keeping an eye on things and gets Lizzie, who hoped, when the phone rang, that this time it might be Paul.

Ernest inquires about her plans, which makes her realize she has none; in that case, he says, would she do him the favor of staying on until he can make an inventory? "We wouldn't want hoodlums breaking in and carting things off."

She is in no hurry to return to the city. Her roommates have rented her room to a Korean medical student for the summer; she will have to stay on Heather's couch and wait tables. And Heather will not be tactful about Paul. Heather will say I told you so, I told you he was an egomaniac. When Heather goes out — Lizzie knows this already — she will sneak to the phone and call Paul's number, only to hang up if he answers; one Saturday she will ride the D train to Brooklyn, on the off-chance of running into him; the next week she'll go to SoHo and wander around the galleries. It won't matter, even, whether she wants him back, or what she thinks of him now; she will be driven to do these things anyway, to play out the obsession until it exhausts her. Ernest is about to offer her more money when she tells him she'll be glad to stay. Then she goes and retrieves Belle's cane, propping it up in the corner by the kitchen door.

But Sophie, when she phones her back, is indignant. "Tell Reichinger to hire a Pinkerton man if he's so worried. You shouldn't be staying in that house alone."

"I'll be fine, honestly."

"You don't sound so good to me."

"I'm all right. Sort of."

"You really loved her so much? Not many people did, you know. How long were you there with her?" When Lizzie tells her, she hoots derisively. "I knew her over fifty years," she says. She recounts the story of how she and Belle first met, at a demonstration in Union Square to protest cuts in the Project. "We had to organize everyone, hand out the signs, decide on the route, everything. The rest of them were hopeless. And then we started walking back to the Village together and wound up all the way down on Wall Street. We didn't want to stop walking, we had too much to say. The next day the same. I must have lost ten pounds the first week I knew her."

She tells Lizzie how she and Belle quarreled about Clay Madden, how Belle nursed him and forgave him and squashed herself down for him until she, Sophie, couldn't stand it anymore. "I never believed it was his art she fell for, not really. It was him, she'd fallen in love with a cowboy, like in the movies. Even his voice was like Gary Cooper, and the way he walked. He was more exotic to her than a Russian prince."

" 'O my America! My new-found-land.' "

"Exactly. Very good."

"But he was a genius."

Sophie snorts. "It's too soon to know that. Once he told me he was a fraud, he couldn't even draw a hand that looked like it had bones in it. No, she wanted to serve a cause, and he was it."

"Maybe that made her happy. At least for a while."

"We didn't think so much about happiness in those days. Yesterday we were happy, when we saw each other again. And then this happened. Phone me tomorrow and tell me how you're doing."

So the next day, after two lanky policemen have shown up with a tape recorder and left again, Lizzie phones to report.

"How did you sleep?" Sophie asks her.

"I didn't at first. But then I turned the radio on and sort of willed myself into oblivion."

"Call Reichinger and tell him you're leaving."

"I don't want to leave. I *like* being here, I *like* feeling her presence."

"I'm starting to think you're a little bit crazy."

"Did I tell you there were nine Maddens hidden in her studio?"

"What? You mean paintings?"

"Yes, but small ones. On paper."

"You better tell Reichinger."

"I did tell him. Yesterday, when I remembered. And he sent two men for them, I think one was a guard. They drove out last night and picked them up. Now I wish I'd really looked at them carefully while they were here. But I didn't feel like it somehow, it almost seemed as though I should just be thinking of her."

"Never mind. Madden's got enough people thinking about him. What did the policemen say?"

"Sam could go to jail," Lizzie says in a rush. "For involuntary manslaughter. Because the accident happened in the course of an illegal assault. Sort of. But it probably won't happen, they said, it hardly ever does in cases like this. He'll just get a slap on the wrist." She lets out her breath. "The thing is, Nina is pregnant. His wife. And she's really nice."

"So who knows what to hope for?"

"Do you think Miss Prokoff would have wanted him to be punished?"

"Don't worry about it. Where she is, it doesn't matter who goes to jail."

"I wish I could meet you in person."

"What do you want to do that for? Forget about me and get on with your life." But she tells Lizzie to call her the next morning, which Lizzie does. On the following evening, she phones and complains that she hasn't heard from Lizzie all day.

In the dingy hall on West 14th Street that Belle had designated for her memorial service, the brief prayers are over. Ernest walks to the podium and clears his throat. Meanwhile, Lizzie and Sophie, who decided jointly not to attend ("I know who we'd find there," Sophie said, "vultures and parasites"), are honoring the occasion on the telephone.

"The minute I woke up this morning," Lizzie says, "I knew something had changed. And then I realized I couldn't feel her presence any more, the house was empty."

"Maybe she'd had enough. Or maybe she went to the funeral to hear what they'd say about her."

What Lizzie really thinks, though she wouldn't say it out loud, is that Belle has left because she knows Lizzie can manage without her now; Lizzie is not so helpless as she was. In the middle of the night, when she couldn't sleep, she fished out the blue notebook she'd brought the first time she came to the house. She wrote down what Belle had said to her that last morning, and how Paul's face was streaked with tears in the studio; she wrote about Paul and Sam climbing the tree, and Mark Dudley's sneer, and Nina clutching Sam's arm as she told him to leave. After an hour her fingers ached from gripping the pen, her eyes were bleary from crying, but when she went back to bed she fell asleep instantly, and slept until morning without dreaming.

Ernest has asked the assembled company of dealers and curators and critics to imagine a different Belle Prokoff from the one they knew — young and poor, undernourished much of the time, living in a fifth-floor walk-up and trying to stay warm by the heat of a gas oven. Painting at night, after she got off work, taking painting classes when she could scrape together the money, always knowing it was the one thing worth doing. "I'm sure she didn't give much thought to comfort, she never did. I'm sure she had a certain scorn, even, for the consolations of this world. It was something else she was after."

"Do you think it would be silly," Lizzie asks, "if we said a prayer for her?"

"You go ahead."

In his loft in Brooklyn, Paul is methodically rolling up canvases, so that they will burn more easily. He is planning to throw them out the window, onto the litter of broken glass in the vacant lot below, and then dig a pit in the sandy soil and make a fire. He likes the simplicity of this scheme, he likes its promise of release: once the paintings are gone, there'll be nothing to hunger after any more, nothing left to brood about. He can walk down the street without hating every bastard whose name is on the plate-glass window of some gallery.

"And then a few years later," Ernest says, "when her own work had finally begun to take off, when she thought she might have found her true direction, she met Clay Madden."

"Couldn't you do it? I only know the Christian ones."
"I never went to *shul* when I was a kid, my father was an atheist. Or when I grew up either."

"There were all sorts of people in the Village in those days who had replaced God with art, but they tended to see it as a purely theoretical matter. They went to the bars and argued, with varying degrees of eloquence, about what they called a higher reality, and that was all they thought was required of them. But she was a primitive, you see, she didn't understand about theoretical allegiances. She thought it was required of her that she keep Clay Madden alive."

"I'll just leave out any references to Jesus."
"It doesn't matter. Say the Hail Mary, anything. Just pray."

"They got diverted, most of them, into trying for ordinary happiness. They forgot about wanting greatness, it was all too difficult, it demanded too much, and there were no rewards. But it never occurred to her that she could do things differently. She never developed much interest in happiness. And that remained true even when the world had begun to reward her in all sorts of ways."

Paul jerks open the window and reaches for the first painting — the homage to Cézanne's mountains. But as he picks it up he feels a tingling in his hands, a flash of memory taking him back to the morning he finished it, three years ago. He'd been up all night, overlaying a circle on a triangle and removing it again, gouging out a series of undulating lines on the lower left; he was craning his neck to watch the sky turn pink and gold over the rubble when suddenly pure joy descended, a stillness like the beginning of the world.

"The longer she lived," Ernest says, "the more obsolete her creed became. Art had come to be seen as something wholly different, a consumable commodity, a species of entertainment. But seeing that happen only made her conviction stronger."

" 'Lord, now lettest thou thy servant depart in peace, according to thy word,' " Lizzie says, in a trembling voice.

"Which brings me to the matter of her will," Ernest says, clearing his throat, and they all sit up straight. It was her final affirmation of faith, he tells them, though he's not really sure about that: it might have been her final act of revenge.

Paul sets the canvas back on the floor, next to the others, and shuts the window. Already he feels a familiar agitation, an awakening hum in his nerves. In an hour, a day, he will be stroking paint on a canvas again. He thinks of all the paintings in all the galleries in the city – so much clutter in the world, and soon he will start making some more. But there's nothing he can do about it; it's what he knows, he doesn't want anything else. Let other people burn his paintings if they want to, after he is dead. There's nothing he can do about that, either.

"She did not leave her Maddens to a museum," Ernest tells them — their chairs creak in unison as they lean towards him — "but to establish a foundation for worthy artists in need. You could say that she left Clay Madden's work to his successors."

A murmur passes along the rows of folding chairs, a sharp inhalation of breath is audible, and then a rising buzz of voices. Ernest presses on. "But you here are all her inheritors. You are responsible for making sure her legacy is preserved. By that I mean not her paintings, or his paintings, but that idea they had of something that existed outside the marketplace, outside fashion and public relations and the whole vast machinery of the world. It may be that it is being honored in places you have never seen, by people you have never heard of, that it has no part in the noise and glitter clamoring for our attention. It is what will survive, what we will return to, after all the rest has been washed away." He bows his head and mumbles, " 'O let the work of our hands be enduring.' "

It's as though he has loosed a whiff of incense into the room, or sung for them an ancient Druid chant; something solemn yet curiously pleasurable has taken place in their consciousness. One of them remembers the first time she stepped inside the Brancacci Chapel; others are suddenly nostalgic for their grandfathers or their old headmasters.

Then Ernest descends from the podium and hurries off. A dealer in lithographs notices the moonstone bracelet on her neighbor's arm; a curator of video art is struck by the handsomeness of the shoes (Italian, hand-sewn leather) he himself is wearing. A young gallery assistant gets out her compact and opens it surreptitiously, worried that the throbbing on her chin means a zit is breaking through. Watching them from his seat in the last row, Mark Dudley gives a knowing smile.